Perilous Days

A Story of Faith and Courage

Brave Hearts Series #1

Kathryn Griffin Swegart

God Bless !

Kathryn Griffin
Swegart

ISBN Print 9781726223928
Cover art credit:
John Folley
www.johnfolley.com

The people who walked in darkness have seen a great light. Upon those who dwelt in the land of gloom a light has shone. You have brought them abundant joy and great rejoicing.

(Is 8:23)

To Colin

Chapter 1

The Ancient Serpent

Germany, 1941.

Dragons exist. Lord of them all is Satan, ancient serpent, there at the dawn of time. Yes, evil dragons exist that lurk just out of view. Here is how it works. You turn your head and they flit away, and you think that all is well in your soul, but they are clever dragons that hover on the edge of consciousness-insidious-waiting to pounce on you, waiting for that pinhole opening, pinholes of doubt, anger, discouragement, hunger, loneliness, and hatred.

Dragons of the mind invaded Germany, enslaving the minds of even good people. Father betrayed son. Neighbor turned against neighbor. And I betrayed a man of integrity, a hero in my life. Let me stop there. I am Felix Culpa Schmidt and here is my story.

One autumn day in 1941, I stood in a wheat field, grain shining under bright sunshine. A farmer swung his scythe, cutting hay for livestock. Oxen stood harnessed to a hay wagon, resigned to their work. Breezes kicked up from northern ridges with warnings that winter snows would soon blanket the land; changes were in the wind. I needed to remember this golden light upon wheat fields and try to shake my heavy heart that grieved over the loss of my grandmother.

On August 2, 1941, we buried Grandmother Schmidt, who had been stricken with influenza. She was buried in a cemetery next to Queen of Peace Church. Trembling aspen trees shaded us from a blistering sun. I lifted my head and thought it strange that aspen leaves shook on windless days. It made me think how little I noticed, how little I knew. Until this moment, I never thought about people dying. I never thought that Grandmother would die, or Grandfather will die. I believed that Mama would never die, so young was she with soft brown hair and sharp eyes that seemed to see everything. Papa would never die, so strong was he from work in the fields. At times, I forgot that he had only one eye, covered by a black patch. On the day of his accident, he ran toward the house, blood streaming down his face. He had been out fencing the pasture and a piece of barbed wire snapped, puncturing his eyeball. The doctor could not save it. Mama said it was God's will. It kept him out of the war. On the day of Grandmother's funeral, my younger brother Willy sat on crab grass growing in the cemetery and picked tiny white flowers that looked like bells. A grasshopper whirred by him and he laughed. Father Mueller uttered the final Amen, and then we stood there like statues until Grandfather said puzzling words. He said, "She is the lucky one. Dark days lie ahead."

Dark days seemed far away on that autumn afternoon, standing on the south German plain. To the north flowed the blue Danube. To the south were the Bavarian Alps. I was young back then, only sixteen, with hair the color of wheat and dark blue eyes. You might say I blended in with my surroundings. I did not tell you that the Black Forest was to our west. Mama always told me that I was growing tall, like those blue spruce. Already, my wrist bones stuck out of my sleeve, and my shoes pinched at the toes. Only on this southern plain did I feel rooted. Never, for even one day, did I desire to leave.

Twilight would soon be upon me, announced by a setting sun. Wheat fields turned to gold. A butterfly drifted overhead in search of wildflowers. How noiseless were those wings, as the butterfly circled above and far away. He sought to find sweet home in a wildflower. A twinge in my heart made me think that we were kindred spirits. That yellow and black swallowtail circled back to me. Straight out of the grass leaped Rolf, my plump German shepherd puppy, but he missed the butterfly and took a tumble. Rolf ran to me on his short puppy legs, tongue flapping. I squatted, and he leaped into my arms.

3

Young man and pup we were in that time before our troubles began. We stepped out of the pasture, and I gazed at my home. The village where I lived was nestled among hills. A church spire rose above clusters of small farms. We strolled along dirt paths; I threw sticks and Rolf searched the tall grass for his treasure. Down we went through gaps in the fir forest until I saw the gray gable of our farmhouse. I heard the swish of the scythe, of father cutting hay. I heard the clatter of pans, of mother baking loaves. Grandmother had been our chief baker. Now Mother took over the task.

Off to the right was a small barn with a smoke stack rising at the roof ridge. Such a familiar sight it was, made from old boards salvaged from decrepit barns, hammered together years ago to build a blacksmith shop for Grandfather's work. I heard the clank of hammer on iron. Grandfather had long since stopped shoeing horses. "Old war wound," he explained simply. A hand grenade had exploded nearby, leaving shrapnel in his leg. His shop smelled of wood smoke. Orange embers burned brightly in the stove. Carefully nailed to the walls were mechanical drawings of bicycle gears, drawn with precision by Grandfather. For many months, he worked long hours on a tricycle for Willy.

"You entered at a momentous time," Grandfather said.

I studied the old man's face. White eyebrows curled down

over his eyes, bright with intelligence and good humor. As Grandfather polished Willy's tricycle, he lifted it off the workbench. "My masterpiece is ready for Sir Willy's first ride. Our little prince deserves royal wheels, leather seat, chrome handlebars, wide pedals. And look at the little bell. Try it."

I pulled the lever. It sounded like chimes, tinkling and musical.

"Keep it a secret now," Grandfather said. "We will give it to him tomorrow after church."

Grandfather squinted at the handlebars, probably looking for smudges. In the process, he discovered a loose bolt. "Hand me that wrench up on the shelf, the small one to the right," he said. As I picked up the wrench, a shiny object caught my eye. It was a metal canister, two inches in length, tucked behind all the tools. I had never noticed it before.

"What is this?" I asked.

"Just a souvenir from the war," he said.

Grandfather never talked about the Great War. I read history books and knew the war lasted from 1914-1918, involved 28 countries and killed 10 million soldiers. I knew that some war veterans had nightmares. Last year I heard him shout in the middle of the night.

Quietly, I slipped out of bed, careful not to step on loose boards that might creak. I opened his bedroom door a crack and saw

Grandfather thrashing in bed. His voice sounded full of fear. I realized that he was transported back to trench combat. I knew this because he jumped up and hid under the bed. "Grandfather, do you need help?" I asked. No answer. Finally, it appeared that the nightmare was over, so he crawled back to bed and drifted off into fitful sleep.

In the daytime, he never talked about machine guns or hand grenades or soldiers dying. All he would talk about were birds. As a private in the German army, his assignment was to train homing pigeons to deliver messages from battlefields back to home base. I handed him the canister.

"What kind of souvenir?"

"Soldiers put messages inside, strapped it to the bird's leg, and let him go. Pigeons can find their way home over hundreds of miles."

"How do they know where to go?"

"It is a mysterious thing. Some people say homing pigeons have something in their brains, something like a compass, to find its way home."

"Oh," I said, not really understanding.

"People have a similar compass, but it is more a spiritual thing."

"Oh," I said. I was beginning to think that life was more mysterious than I had imagined. As you will see as events unfold, that is an understatement.

Chapter 2

The Muenster Lion

The sun appeared above the eastern wood, thick with pointed evergreens. Rising higher, sunlight transfigured our village. Rolf and I walked to church, but I found no joy in this glorious sight. I said a prayer in my head, not knowing if it left my brain and went to heaven. *Are you up there, God? Grandmother is dead. I prayed for her to live. God did not answer my prayer, maybe there is no…* I stopped praying. For one thing, it sounded more like a complaint than a prayer. If I complained to God and there was a God, I was in trouble. If there was no God, prayer did not matter. Logically speaking, nothing would matter. That was my thought for the day. Yet it was my duty to serve as an altar boy at Mass. I turned the last curve and saw Father Mueller unlock the church doors. Rolf bolted ahead, jumped up, and plastered his dirty paws on Father Mueller's black pants. The priest crouched down and patted those pointy ears. Abruptly, Rolf sat down, wagging his tail, creating an arc in the dirt.

"Maybe some of your joy will rub off on me, squirmy puppy. Today of all days, I need it," he said. That brown and black tail stopped wagging. Rolf and I waited for an explanation. That was soon to come, not gently, but more like a sledgehammer to the head. As we entered the church, only a red lamp at the tabernacle lit the darkness. My black cassock and white surplice hung neatly in the closet. I slipped them on and went out to light candles. Villagers began to arrive. As they did every Sunday, my family sat in the front pew. I set out linens, filled cruets, one with water and another with red wine. All was ready for Mass, but my mind was far away. All I could do was go through the motions.

"It is time," Father Mueller said.

I rang a brass bell to announce the start of Mass, and the people slowly came to their feet. Father Mueller kissed the altar and began opening prayers. "*In nomine Patris, et Filii, et Spiritus Sancti. Amen.* I did not hear a word of the Old Testament nor the New Testament nor the Gospel. A sunbeam slanted down through the window. In happier days, sunbeams made me think of the Holy Spirit. Today that did not happen. Father Mueller began his sermon.

"My dear brothers and sisters in Christ, we live in a time of profound evil, evil that pierces the heart. Our beloved homeland, once a holy nation, is now ruled by a man some consider an antichrist. Many of us have had suspicions about the clandestine actions of Adolph Hitler. Now we know that the elderly and disabled are under attack. Adolph Hitler calls them 'useless eaters' who must die for the good of our country. No longer can I be silent. I am not alone. Our courageous bishop of Muenster, Graf von Galen, now speaks out."

I looked at Willy. Neighbors had used the word "disabled" to describe him. To me, he was just my brother. We played games together. Sometimes I teased him, but not often. When he cried, I felt terrible. People said we looked alike. We both had straight blond hair. There was a resemblance, except for the eyes. Willie had upward-turning eyes. My parents explained that Willy had trouble learning and would always live at home. That didn't sound so terrible to me. A new thought made me shudder. Would Hitler label my five-year-old brother a "useless eater?"

Father Mueller held up the bishop's leaflet and began to read.

This secret program to kill innocent citizens of the Reich is against God's commandments. It is against the law of nature and against the system of justice in Germany. These are our brothers and sisters! How can we be expected to live if the measure of our lifespan is economic productivity? We must not use force, but spiritual and moral opposition. Be strong. Be steadfast.

At that moment, rocks crashed through the church windows,

spraying shattered glass on the floor. Loud chanting erupted. "Stop the treason!" Father Mueller grabbed the processional cross and bolted down the aisle. His green vestments fluttered like a great bird. Young men of the Hitler Youth Corps, official youth organization of the Nazi party, stood at the doorway. On my 14th birthday, the Nazi government forced me to join. Their gang leader for this act of terrorism was Rudolf Heck. Every week we gathered to learn slogans and read propaganda leaflets-the intent was to make us good Nazis. Rudolf memorized every word of every Nazi reading. He confronted Father Mueller.

"Stop the lies!" he yelled.

"I tell the truth! Bishop Galen speaks out against the evil practices of Adolph Hitler," Father Mueller shouted.

At these words, they formed a ring around Father Mueller. Rudolph spoke. "Germany is rising out of the ashes of the Great War. Adolph Hitler is our glorious leader. He leads us out of starvation and poverty. And you, a lowly priest, dare speak out against him? You are a traitor to our cause." As the circle drew tighter around Father Mueller, Rudolph continued his tirade. "From now on, you will submit every sermon for our approval."

Father Mueller's voice trembled with anger. "Never! I do not follow a corrupt leader. I follow the Lord Jesus and act as a shepherd for His people. I will not lead them astray. I will speak the truth against these crimes against humanity." He swirled away from the leader and used the cross to push them out of the way. Before the Nazis could act, parishioners formed a human shield and stood in front of Father Mueller. I stood behind my parents, hoping no intruder saw me.

The Nazi youth formed a line and raised their arms in salute. "Heil Hitler!" they shouted in unison. As they turned to leave, Rudolph called out. "We will be back. When we do, we will throw you in a concentration camp, like we have done to hundreds of priests. Many have been executed. Every citizen of the Third Reich must be of one mind. That mind is the mind of Adolph Hitler."

It is not every day that Mass is interrupted by a death threat. I figured at this point, we all would go home. That is not what happened. Father Mueller went back to the altar. "My dear people, we will not be intimidated by these thugs. Be strong. Be steadfast in the Lord Jesus Christ." He took out a handkerchief and wiped his brow. "We will now recite the creed."

When Mass was over, we gathered outside church. Father Mueller put his arm on Papa's shoulder and guided him behind an oak tree. It looked like a secret meeting. As the priest talked, Papa appeared to be in great distress, shaking his head in disagreement. I inched closer to eavesdrop. Father Mueller handed Papa a piece of paper. The priest raised his voice. "You must take this desperate action or Willy will die."

I felt a tug on my trousers. Willy raised his arms. I picked him up and gave him a hug, tighter than ever before. "We will protect you, don't worry," I whispered. "Come on. Let's walk home: you, me, and Rolf."

Willy held my hand; I knew that his hand was different from mine. My fingers were straight and strong with calluses on the palms, formed from years of pitching hay and shoveling manure; now they looked as much a part of my hands as knuckles. Willy had soft hands with bent fingers and pliable muscles, fingers that could bend into a V-shape and somehow not hurt. Neighbors thought his mind was slow, but I did not share this opinion. He saw things adults never noticed. On that dirt road, he found a rock and moved it. Immediately, ants scattered, not all of them, only some; others remained back and stood guard over tiny rice grains.

"Eggs," Willy said.

"Right. Those are ant eggs."

We watched ants for a long time, an activity I would not have done if Willy had not been with me. He taught me to be patient, to observe ants guarding their larvae at risk of death, for we were giants who could kill them with one stomp. Of course, we did not do that. Willy was too gentle, too kind, and the only person I ever knew who smiled at ants. Whenever Willy smiled, he turned to look me square in the eye; it was his way of sharing happiness, of wanting to see other people smile, even if we did not feel like smiling. Crickets sang in fields of tall grass that lined the road home. Willy could not resist that song. We crawled into the field, watching and waiting. Blades of grass moved, and in this parting of blades, we saw a shiny black cricket. In Willy's quiet world, I saw nature with new eyes: I saw crickets with muscular hind legs covered with prickles and near the feet were five spines, two were longer, so I surmised they were for capturing insects. I watched the cricket crouch, pull his legs together, and leap out of sight.

Willy rolled over and gazed up at the sky, at clouds soft and white, bathed in sunlight, drifting slowly, casting shadows over wildflowers, over butterflies, and over us. As clouds passed, seconds of darkness hit my face, but made me think about the world, of what is real that we see and what is real that we cannot see. Darker clouds blanketed the sky. I thought more about Grandfather's words at the funeral. I decided not to worry. After all, I was only 16 and lived in a safe place, in a home filled with the smells of cut grass, fresh bread, and wood fires. Nothing terrible could happen to me.

Chapter 3

Bells

We arrived home to the smell of gingerbread. On Sunday, Mama always made gingerbread. Before sunrise, she was in the kitchen mixing flour with a wooden spoon and beating eggs until they bubbled up to a yellow froth. On dark days to come, I pictured the kitchen, and that memory comforted me. It had whitewashed walls and rough-hewn wooden beams across the ceiling. The floor was made of sturdy oak hammered together with iron nails that Grandfather had forged in his shop. The only fancy decoration was a large wooden window; each pane had diamond-shaped clear glass with the frame painted in rose colors, a wedding present given to my grandparents. Bright red geraniums sat on each window sill.

Mama cut the warm gingerbread into squares, large chunks for "my boys," placing them on pottery plates. Willy climbed onto his stool and waited patiently to say grace. That was hard because he was hungry, but he did it. However, something was strange about the gingerbread. As I took my first bite, I saw that the bottom layer was burned, leaving black crumbs on the plate, crumbs that looked like ashes. Mama never burned gingerbread. She turned and looked out the wedding window onto distant hills. Mama looked at something she could not see.

Willy slipped off his stool and pulled open the heavy door, letting morning sun stream onto the oak floors. He stopped to look at Mama's garden. It was a flower garden she planted one rainy day in April, digging deeply into the soil, filling each hole with ashes from the wood stove. In the summer, we watched a parade of colors, of pale blue forget-me-nots, purple phlox, scarlet roses along the edge, white chrysanthemum that she called Baby's Tears. Willy liked to watch bumblebees crawl down blossoms and back up, flying overhead with yellow pollen covering their back legs.

"Willy, come here and see what I made for you," Grandfather called and gestured at the tricycle covered in a blanket. "I will count to three. When I say three, pull off the blanket. Ready? One-two-THREE!"

Off came the blanket, revealing his tricycle, glistening in sunlight. First, he hugged the tricycle, and then he hugged Grandfather.

He settled onto the leather seat, ringing the bell over and over. His legs were too short to reach the pedal. Grandfather could fix it by bolting wooden blocks to the pedals.

"Help your brother," Grandfather said.

As I pushed Willy along, a man walked toward us. It was Father Mueller with his head down, deep in thought. He looked up at Willy and smiled.

"Pedal hard. Get those legs strong," he said. "Can I ring your bell?"

Willy tapped the bell.

"That means yes," I said.

Father Mueller pulled the lever. "Happiest sound I've heard in weeks."

"Welcome Father. I am relieved you are here, "Grandfather said. "My son is in the house."

Father Mueller gave Grandfather a bear hug. After that, they went inside to meet Papa. Earlier in the day, I had been warned that they would talk about 'matters of grave importance.' That was the expression that Papa used this morning. I was glad to stay outside and play with Willy. I liked to be in Willy's world where all people were kind, and there was no sorrow. Playtime plunged us into faraway lands where white knights triumphed over black knights.

"What do you want to play?" I asked. Willy pointed at yellow leaves that blanketed the ground. We scooped up armfuls, piled them high, and fell backwards. Leaves floated down, drifting like boats on a calm ocean. If only we could stay there forever, feeling safe in our hiding place. That was not to be. Father came out of the house and waved to me.

"Come here," Papa called. "Felix, we are going on a trip. When the sun sets, we will go under cover of night."

We brushed leaves off our clothes and stared up at father, who was holding one small suitcase.

"Where are we going?" I asked.

"Willy is going to a safe place until the war is over."

Fog rolled over my mind, making it difficult for me to think. "Am I to stay at this place too?"

Papa shook his head. "Someday you will understand. For now, Willy must stay at Our Lady of Sorrows Convent. Mother Amelia and the nuns will take good care of him."

At this news, I did an unmanly thing; I cried. My tears made Willy burst into tears. He did not know what was happening, but he could sense fear. Mama turned away to conceal her tears. Grandfather pinched tears away from his nose. Father Mueller hugged Papa. Rolf ran around them like a crazy dog. He did not understand either.

"You must hide evidence that Willy ever lived here. The Nazi secret police—the despicable Gestapo—will come to find him. Give away his clothes, his bed, everything," Father Mueller said.

"What about his tricycle?" Grandfather asked.

"The Gestapo confiscates forbidden books, books written by

Jewish authors and others, and then they burn them. People bury books and precious belongings in hidden places. You should bury that tricycle. It is obvious that you built it for a disabled person."

Father Mueller opened a bottle of holy water and blessed Willy on the forehead. He turned to Papa. "Go under cover of night. Take the dog. If there are spies, Rolf will hear them. Here is a map to the convent. It is well-hidden, so few know that it exists."

That night, we left and set out on narrow paths through stands of tall trees. Barely visible among the treetops was a full moon, hanging like a bright beacon in the night sky. Mile after mile, we trod. I felt as if in a trance, lulled into memories of days now past. *Grandmother stood in a sunlit kitchen, her hands shuffled over the breadboard, kneading dough. There she stood, in a floury apron, and dusted the board, until she sat in a chair, tired so soon.*

"I am getting old. I cannot stand like I used to." She said and wiped a lock of hair off her face. A blotch of flour landed on her forehead, like ashes on Ash Wednesday. She looked so real in this daydream, I desired to be with her.

We came to a river full of foam and stones, where Papa paused to study the map. Willy awoke and wiggled out of Papa's arms. As he always did, Rolf licked Willy's cheek, which made him giggle.

"Almost there. Down one more hill," Papa said.

We walked the rugged trail down a valley, over a moist forest floor that had a musky smell. No light penetrated the dense forest ceiling. Ghosts seemed to lurk behind trees, lurching at me with evil fingers. Rolf trotted beside me; his ears twitched at every sound. Leaves twirled in tiny dances, but I did not hear the crunch of footsteps, those of evil men. As we came to a clearing, the path narrowed and appeared strewn with white stones. Moonlight reflected off the stone path, shining like bright snow, leading us to Our Lady of Sorrows Convent. It was a grey stone building with bell tower and chimney stuck in the middle of a slate roof. Antique, it was, centuries old as evidenced by moss growing along the walls. An order of Poor Clare nuns hid away from the world and prayed. Papa picked up Willy and pulled the cord of a bell hanging beside the door. From behind the door came the sound of swishing robes and urgent whispering. As the door opened, Mother Amelia stood before us. I was struck by her appearance as if I saw a vision. A long black robe came to her ankles. It was made of course cloth and was frayed at the cuffs. White cords and rosary beads hung from her waist. Around her face was a white kerchief, wide enough to cover her chin. Her face was partly hidden. She smiled slightly.

"Welcome. Father Mueller has told us your story. Now, this must be Willy." She gently touched his arm. Willy snuggled into Papa's shoulder. "Go quickly. Spies are everywhere. I pray that you were not followed. Understand that you must not visit. Know that Willy is safe." Without warning, she turned to me. "We live in perilous times, especially young men going to war. Have you been confirmed?"

"I have."

"Good. You will need that special strength of the Holy Spirit. You will run into deadly obstacles. Fortitude will be necessary." She made a fist to show her own strength. "Our nuns will pray for you. Pray to your guardian angel. He will protect you," she held out her arms to Willy. "Do not be afraid, Willy. We love you, little one. All the sisters feel this way."

Willy clung to Papa who kissed his cheek. "It is time to go with Mother Amelia. We will see you soon." He handed him over to Mother Amelia. Willy's face turned red as he cried hard and struggled to get away from her. With a swirl of long black robes, they disappeared into the cloister. Up in the tower, an ancient bell tolled solemnly, calling the nuns to vespers.

It felt like a funeral. Willy was gone, perhaps forever.

Chapter 4

Hans

On Saturday, I trudged through a blizzard that caked my winter jacket with snow. Miraculously, Rolf and I were on time for winter camping with the Hitler Youth Corps. In 1936, the Nazi government made membership in the Hitler Youth Corps mandatory. Every week I attended meetings. Hans Scholl was our squad leader, a young man soon to enter medical studies at the University of Munich. He looked the part of a leader with straight posture and alert eyes. Many badges were attached to his uniform shirt. A patch worn on the upper portion of his shoulder was black with two white diamonds in the center, indicating his rank as squad leader, squad number 753. Pinned to his brown shirt was an array of awards; Golden Leader's Sports Badge, Marksmanship Proficiency Badge, and Youth Member Honor Badge, trimmed in gold.

"Strap on your snowshoes, men, we are going hiking," he announced and swung a rifle over his shoulder. We all hoisted canvas backpacks that contained water, bread, and change of socks. Our hike took us deep into the forest. Rolf plowed through deep drifts on his short legs. Snow caked onto his pointy muzzle. He shook snow off his fur and looked up at me with eyes that shone with excitement.

"You think this is like heaven, you silly dog," I said and threw a snowball. He caught it in his mouth. Rolf did not care about the weather. To him it was cool and refreshing. Temperatures dipped below freezing as an icy wind blasted our faces. With each step, I knew what brought us out into a blizzard. We had to be tough and ready for war. We may be assigned to the Russian front where temperatures dipped to 50 below zero.

As the morning wore on, I felt numbness in my toes. Ice stuck to my eyelids. I pulled the wool scarf over my mouth and breathed warm air onto my cheeks. Still we forged on through snowdrifts. Finally, we came to a grove of birch trees and stopped. Hans pulled out his rifle and made a motion for the squad to crouch and be silent. A snowshoe hare sat on his haunches near a thicket. Barely visible in the snow, his white winter fur fluffed up in a gust. Camouflaged by layers of snow, we remained hidden from the hare. Hans raised his rifle and the hare took off. He was light with big feet that enabled him to skim over the snow. Hans took aim and squeezed the trigger. Down the hare went in a splash of snow. That night we dug a shallow pit and used paper bark from a birch tree and dead twigs to start a crackling fire. Sparks shot up through the night sky and smoke rose through falling snowflakes. Hans roasted the hare on a stick. We ate hot meat with bare hands, like real soldiers. On that night by the campfire, the prospect of war was a romantic adventure.

Squad 753 met the following Monday for an education meeting. "Welcome, my friends," Hans said, his voice robust and sincere. "Tonight, we will finish making the flag of our squad. As we hold this flag proudly, it will be different from all flags made by Hitler Youth squads. But first, I am required to show you the following film. It contains information I do not..." Hans stopped himself abruptly. Silence hung over us like dense fog. Hans appeared to struggle inwardly, looking at the young boys who eagerly awaited his next words.

"Never mind. Let us continue with the program, *Triumph of the Will*. That is the title of the movie I will show you. It is about the 1936 rally at Nuremburg to honor Adolph Hitler on his birthday. Hans paused to clear his throat. "I was at this rally along with 400,000 other Germans."

Hans stood next to the heavy metal 16mm film projector. He threaded the film into a spool, through rollers that fed into another large spool. With overhead lights off, the projector clattered into motion, displaying images on a white wall. A small plane flew through clouds and tipped its wings to reveal swastikas--it was Hitler's private plane. Below was a stadium jammed with thousands of spectators. Spotlights aimed into the heavens, shooting white lights on the plane as it descended. Thousands of Nazis gathered, including the Hitler Youth Corps. Row upon row of German youth stood erect, awaiting the words of their leader.

The narrator said. "*Germans gathered in the stadium before the Fuehrer to show him what they are made of, that they belong to him. The Fuehrer— their Fuehrer— stood before the microphone to speak to them. Every time Adolph Hitler tried to begin, the endless cheers of 'Heil' roar again.*"

Adolph Hitler gazed out on the sea of uniformed Hitler Youth, Gestapo, and storm troopers. His dark brown hair, cut in the shape of a bowl, was parted neatly to the side. He wore a small mustache that looked like a brush. I could not watch anymore. I picked up Rolf, feeling the puppy's heart beat against my own. Light from the film flickered on the faces of the squad. Rudolph Heck sat in the front row. It appeared like he was being hypnotized. Hans closed his eyes while *Triumph of the Will* droned on. The narrator continued "*...spectators and the Fuehrer himself were overcome with exhilaration and a fervor for which there are no words. Everything else is forgotten. One thought only, one fire has consumed us all.*"

That was the end. Hans switched off the projector and

everything went black. Minutes passed before the lights came on. Now Hans did not speak, but looked at his Hitler Youth squad, eager to know more about this new Germany. Imperceptibly, he shook his head. *No fervor here, no exhilaration for the Fuehrer in this man,* I thought. Hans chose his words carefully, "I have nothing to say about this propaganda film. We now proceed to the next item on our agenda. Tonight, we will finish our squad banner. Tomorrow, dozens of squads will meet in town square for inspection by our superiors."

With a flourish, he held the banner high. Cut from colorful cloth, a mythical creature like a peacock seemed to fly out of a fire, his yellow eyes gleaming, and red legs lifting out of orange flames. It was a Phoenix, the symbol of new life rising out of ashes, different from all other squad banners. This disturbed me. Any deviance from uniformity, from the iron fist of the Hitler Youth Corps, brought punishment. It would be wise to keep distance from all things different. At squad review, I resolved to stand in back, hidden from all scrutiny.

"I now choose the young man who will carry our banner," Hans scanned the squad. "Felix, you have perfect attendance at our meetings. Even your dog has been at every meeting. Rolf is smart. You have trained him well. In fact, I informed my superiors that he would make a fine war dog, a dog trained to help our troops. Felix, you are a leader. That is why you will carry our banner."

"But, sir…" I stammered.

"No dispute. Carry our banner proudly, the banner of squad 753. Tomorrow night, we will march in a torch lit parade with other squads. Dismissed."

As evening of the following day drew near, I went about chores in silence. Rolf followed everywhere. After milking the cows, we went to the well for water. It was an old well with a wooden bucket tied to a windlass. I cranked the handle, let go and watched it plummet. I leaned over the edge and yelled. "Help!" The well returned my voice, no longer a boy's voice, but deep, like that of a man. Soon I would be sixteen. Willy was gone. Grandmother was gone. Soon Rolf could be gone. Rolf gazed up at me with bright eyes, one ear up, the other flopped over.

"Perhaps I have trained you too well," I said. With a heavy heart, I trudged back to the house carrying two buckets of water, Rolf close at my heels.

On the streets of our village, regiments of Hitler Youth gathered for a torchlit parade. Villagers propped photographs of Hitler up against window panes. Nazi flags hung from window sills and stuck to wet brick buildings. I held our banner in front of my face. Perhaps my identity would go unnoticed. On each side were boys carrying torches. Ahead was a military band playing martial music on pipes and drums. I glanced up and saw women waving at the columns of marching boys. An old woman pointed at me. I wanted to throw the banner down and run. I lowered the banner and stared at Hans, who marched briskly in front of me. Abruptly Hans ordered, "Halt."

In the town square, squads lined up in neat rows awaiting inspection by Herbert Schneider, a high-ranking official in the Hitler Youth Corps. The man looked like Hitler with a brush moustache and neatly cropped hair. Schneider walked slowly up and down rows of uniformed boys, tapping a small riding whip on the palm of his hand. Schneider stopped and stared in disbelief at our Phoenix banner.

"Who is responsible for this traitorous flag?" he yelled and ripped the banner away. Schneider whipped my arm, tearing the uniform. "Leave him alone!" shouted Hans. With an explosive burst of speed, Hans ran at Schneider and punched him in the face. Schneider fell to the ground. A wave of shock, like electricity pulsing through wire, shot through me. Dire thoughts gripped my mind. Hans was guilty of insubordination. He could be thrown into the rat-infested barracks of a concentration camp, there left to die.

Hans clicked his heals and stood at attention. "These young men are under my instruction. Our banner was not their idea, it was mine. As all Germans in Nazi Germany, they were acting out of strict obedience. Punish me, not them."

In the orange light of torches, I saw blood dripping from Schneider's nose. It created a puddle in the dirt. Schneider rose to his feet and caught dark liquid bubbling out of his nostrils. He took a handful of blood and smeared it on Hans until his face was covered from forehead to chin.

"I have marked a swastika on your face with my own blood. Our hearts beat for Adolph Hitler. There is no room for deviant thoughts, deviant words, deviant acts." With those words, he stripped Hans of his badges. Hans did not flinch at the humiliation. He simply walked away. Almost like a ghost, he turned a corner and was gone. As Schneider spun on his heels, I scooped up the squad leader badge and tucked it in my pocket. The image of Hans and his bloody face stayed with me that night and for many nights over many long years.

Chapter 5

Blizzards

I tossed and turned that night, falling asleep just as gray light signaled the start of another day. Winds howled around the farmhouse, rattling windows. A fire roared in the fireplace. I stuck my head out from under the blankets and saw snow in white twirls pounding the window panes. Quickly, I got up and dressed. Rolf hopped out of bed and trotted over to the fireplace. Mama put wood on the fire and drew a shawl around her shoulders.

"I have bad feelings about this winter," she said, breaking ice from the water pail. "the wrath of God is unleashed on us. I feel it in my bones."

Papa pushed through the door with an armload of wood; piles of snow blew in with him. He dumped the wood into a box and warmed his hands by the stove. No one said anything. It felt like a matter of survival. We wrapped ourselves up in woolen blankets and ate hot cornmeal from pottery bowls. Grandfather sat in his rocking chair and reached for the radio dial. The radio was in a wooden cabinet with a speaker in front.

"Time to earn my jail sentence," he said and tuned into the

British Broadcasting Company radio station.

"Father, you know that station is forbidden. We are required by law to listen only to Nazi radio sets," Papa said.

Grandfather did not hear well out of his left ear. At times, it seemed that he used that as an excuse to pursue his own will, leaving it impossible to know what he actually heard. Reception of the signal was scratchy. A red line on the radio dial needed to be set exactly on 89.5-British radio. The old man squinted as he fiddled with the dial. Finally, the crackling ceased. A British announcer translated the news into German. *Reports from the Russian front bring bad news to Adolph Hitler. Severe winter weather has battered German troops. Freezing blizzards and blinding winds have swept across the eastern plains of Russia. Many of Hitler's army suffered from frigid temperatures and starvation. In just one day, 14,000 German soldiers endured frostbite, requiring amputation of limbs. Many died days later. Hitler will soon be forced to call up young men, some as young as sixteen, from the Hitler Youth Corps.*

Papa spoke harshly, "Grandfather, why do you turn on foreign radio stations? The British, with their top hats and umbrellas, they are trying to make Germans lose heart by telling us lies. It will be a much different story on the official radio set given to us by the Nazi government." Papa turned on the short-wave radio. A Nazi announcer, triumphantly proclaimed, *"On the morning of June 22, 1941, our German army launched the greatest land invasion in the history of warfare. Three million men thrust into Soviet territory to conquer this immense land mass. Swift victory followed. German troops destroyed 4,000 Soviet aircraft and conquered Kiev. Soon Moscow will be flying the Nazi flag.*

Papa clicked off the radio. "Did you hear? We are winning the war. Soon the conflict will end, and our men will come home."

Grandfather shook his head. "That is what you want to believe because you do not want Felix to go off to war. That report is from six months ago. Now we have two enemies to fight: the Russians and the Russian winter. Our enemy digs in with a tenacity the generals underestimated. Now our men fight with frostbitten fingers and toes. Hitler will draft young men, for young men foolishly plunge into battle thinking thy will never die, thinking they are immortal. Do not believe Nazi reports. They are liars and they murder their own people."

Papa stared into the fireplace. As he sighed deeply, emotions flitted across his face. He lifted the cast iron kettle that hung over the fire and poured Grandfather hot tea. Silently, Papa picked up his hat and hung it over the photograph of Adolph Hitler, required to be hung in every German home. I glanced nervously out the window. If a Nazi saw this act of disrespect, my father could be sent away to jail.

Papa gazed into the fire. "How can one man spread such evil?"

No answer came.

The blizzard raged on as we hid out, buried in snowdrifts. That is the way winter started; that was the way it continued. All was monotony until one day, we heard a knock on the door. An older boy dressed in the brown uniform of the Hitler Youth Corps stood at attention. "I am looking for Felix Culpa Schmidt."

"That is me," I said.

"I have a letter for you from the Fuehrer."

"Me? From the Fuehrer?"

"Orders await you. Heil Hitler," he saluted. "I will see you at recruitment headquarters." With that, he marched down the road like he was in his own private parade.

I slipped my finger under a wax seal and held the envelope up to lamplight. It was from the war department and read, *Report for a medical examination on January 11th at ten o'clock. Bring your birth certificate.* We all stared at the fire. Not a word was spoken. I looked at Mama's face. Tears brimmed over and hung on her long lashes. Papa stacked a heavy log on the embers. It smothered the hot coals, causing smoke to fill the fireplace. This was strange. Papa was an expert at building fires. Never would he be so careless. I sneaked a glance at him. Even in the orange glow, his face appeared ashen, deep in thought.

"Papa, the fire is almost out," I said.

"Indeed, it is," he said and stoked the fire with a bundle of twigs. "My son, you are going off to war. We will write, but I do not know if these letters will ever get to you. If they do, the Gestapo will open them. I will inform you of what is happening about Willy, but it will be in code. Fox means Gestapo. As for the rest, I will still use code, but it will be clear to you. Understand?"

"Yes, Papa."

"Rest assured, we will pray for you every day. Always pray to your guardian angel."

I pulled a blanket over my face so that he could not see my look of skepticism. Guardian angels were figments of the imagination. As a young man going to war, I had to face hard reality. I had to face machine guns and bombs. I could not afford to rely on fairy tales.

One week later, I reported to the local recruitment office. It was a bank once run by a Jewish family, the Rothschilds, who had fled the country to avoid Nazi persecution. When I arrived, neighborhood teenagers stood nervously in line. I saw

Rudolph Heck standing at military attention, like he was already in the army. He glanced at me, smirking in his usual way. Behind him was a man with graying hair. Three makeshift examining rooms were set up in the lobby. A nurse dressed in white stood at the front of the line and called out names.

"Alfons Heinz, Room C," she began.

"Herbert Shultz, Room B." The gray-haired man stepped forward.

Rudolph whispered to me, "They take anyone, old men, and even stupid boys like you. We are all going to the Russian front. That is for sure."

Felix Schmidt, Room A, with Dr. Norkus," she said.

I clutched my birth certificate and pulled away a sheet that served as a door. Doctor Norkus did not greet me, only gestured for me to sit. My eyes focused on a newspaper placed on the corner of his desk. The headlines were in large, bold print. **EXECUTED!** As Norkus studied my birth certificate, I read the first sentence. *Three university students were executed for distributing leaflets that betrayed the glorious leadership of our beloved Fuehrer, Adolph Hitler.* Norkus slapped his hand on the desk.

"Wake up, boy!" he said sharply. He slipped paper on a clipboard and wrote *Felix Culpa Schmidt* at the top.

"Strip to your underwear and step on the scale," he said.

On one line, he wrote 140 pounds and scribbled on a notepad the word, *passed*. The doctor placed his stethoscope on my chest and listened to my heartbeat. My heart beat rapidly due to the extreme sense of terror that gripped me. The newspaper headline added to my worries. *Who would kill university students for distributing leaflets?* I knew the answer. Norkus scribbled on the medical checklist, *passed*. I desperately wanted to flunk something. If I believed in God, I would have asked Him to flunk me out of the army.

"Breathe deeply. In and out." His handwriting looked exactly the same each time-*passed*. Norkus took out a scope and checked eyes, then ears. *Passed. Passed.* Dr. Norkus pressed a round stamp onto an ink pad. In bold red ink it said *PASSED*.

"You are fit for duty in the German army," Norkus said.

I waited for the fateful words. Surely, I was going to the Russian front. Instead, Dr. Norkus picked up a letter sitting on a small table next to him.

"You own a German Shepherd. Correct?" he asked.

"Yes, sir."

"I have a letter signed by Colonel Dubach assigning you to the canine corps training center in Frankfurt. You and the dog report to the training center in one week." Dr. Norkus handed me the official document. "Now get out of here. I have no time for boys staring stupidly at a piece of paper. Next recruit, Rudolph Heck"

He bumped into me and asked, "Russian front?"

"No. Not yet anyway."

From behind the sheet, Dr. Norkus said to Rudolph, "Strip to your underwear and step on the scale." We all were part of the German war machine. At least for me, I marched off to war with Rolf by my side.

Chapter 6

Dog Squad

Frankfurt, Germany February 1943. Under light drizzle, Rolf and I stood at the train station. Families crowded around young soldiers going off to war. My family huddled close to me. Grandfather hugged me, all the while mumbling something about war being insanity, war making men crazy. Mama hugged me tightly. Papa shook my hand. Abruptly, he pulled me close and whispered a prayer.

"May the Lord send good men to protect you," he prayed. Our farewell was broken by the shout of a commandant, "Families leave now. The train is coming soon."

My family was absorbed in the crowd as the families moved off the railroad platform. Soldiers pushed them away with rifles until they were out of sight. Light rain began to fall. I turned my face to the dark sky and let raindrops mingle with my tears. It was the loneliest moment of my life. Rolf pulled at the leash and I snapped out of my trance. When I turned to wait for the train, a bright color caught my eye. It was a red poster plastered to a wall at the depot.

"Come on Rolf, let's check this out," I said, trying to pull myself together. The poster was an announcement from the Nazi government.

Sentenced to death for high treason:

Christoph Probst, age 24

Hans Scholl, age 25

Sophie Scholl, age 22

The sentence has already been carried out.

I breathed in sharply and gently touched the name of Hans Scholl. My skin crawled with tension. I reached out for the wall to steady myself. With back flat against the wall, I slid down and my head drooped. Hans— I could see his face, exuberant in the snowy woods, teaching us courage. Courage. That was what I needed. I reached in my pocket and pulled out his leadership badge. At this point, heavy rain beat down on me. I held the badge close to my heart and whispered, *Hans Scholl; I want to be brave like you.*

Suddenly I was aware of a man standing over me. It was a Gestapo soldier probably in search of German citizens guilty of political crimes. At the sight of his black knee-high boots and gray uniform, tension throbbed in my temples. The man's face was white, marked by a long pointy nose and small black eyes. "Are you one of them?" he asked sharply.

"What are you talking about?" I asked.

"One of the White Rose, that traitorous group bent on tearing down the Nazi government and our beloved fuehrer."

"I am not part of this group."

"Did you know any of these three traitors?" he asked, pointing at the poster.

"I did not know them."

"I saw you look at the poster. You touched a name and you began to cry. You knew Hans Scholl. Tell the truth."

"I did not know him."

"Prove it. Denounce this group and this man."

My heart buzzed with fear; slimy words sprang from my mouth. "I renounce the White Rose as enemies of the state. I condemn Hans Scholl, Sophie Scholl, and Christoph Probst."

At that, the man snapped his heels together, saluted Hitler, and walked away.

In all the wet of my tears and the rain, I felt a damp nose press against my cheek. Rolf looked at me with sad brown eyes. It appeared as if he felt my sorrow. It is hard to remember how long we sat there in the rain. In the distance I heard a train whistle and the clatter of wheels on the track. As the locomotive slowed to a halt, clouds of steam puffed onto the platform. I boarded in silence with other recruits and found seats behind two men wearing swastika armbands.

They whispered to each other, but I heard.

"I attended University of Munich. How impossible it is for me to believe of such treachery. Students painted graffiti on walls, 'Down with Hitler!'" said the one, shaking his head. "Called themselves the White Rose. These traitors threw leaflets down from an upper hall to the atrium below and ran away. Fortunately, a janitor saw and reported them." He grunted in disgust.

At these words, my brain shut down. A wave of nausea rose in my throat. Only with deep swallowing did I force it back down. The German countryside whizzed by in a blur. "Just like my life," I said to Rolf. Alone in our railroad compartment, I stared out the window, Rolf with his muzzle on my lap. Night fell, engulfing us in darkness. The train rumbled on and on, over bridges, through meadows, past lonely forests far from home. In the peaceful rhythm of Rolf's breathing, I felt comfort. This dog had such trust in me. He did not know that we were going to war. No, life according to Rolf was an adventure, pure and simple. His tail thumped on the seat. I squeezed the badge in my hand and fell asleep.

Dawn broke as we pulled into the station. Frankfurt was an ancient city with a skyline of church spires and smoke stacks from factories. I saw a German soldier standing on the train platform, smoking a cigarette. He inhaled deeply, like this was his only pleasure in life. Rolf and I emerged from the train. The man walked over to me.

"I am Herbert Metelmann; your papers, please," he said, flicking the cigarette away. Metelmann studied the papers carefully. "This is highly unusual. Rolf must be very smart and have a sensitive nose."

"Yes, sir, he has been that way since he was eight weeks old," I replied.

"Interesting. Very well then, you are assigned to the casualty dog training center. Rolf is to be a sanitary dog, trained to find injured soldiers in the battlefield. Report for duty at seven a.m. sharp. His first lesson is to identify the German uniform. He must learn to find only German soldiers."

Rolf's nose worked as he sifted through the new smells of the kennels. I crouched down and put my hand through the bars of his cage. Rolf leaned against the cage and sighed heavily. No soft bed to sleep on, only a concrete floor. As the sun set, I went to the barracks, trying not to think of Rolf surrounded by dogs howling out of fear and loneliness. When I arrived at the barracks, I found a brown paper package sitting on my cot. I tore open the package and found an infantryman's uniform. It was dark green, with matching field cap, and trousers. Reluctantly, I put on the uniform and stared at myself in a full-length mirror. The jacket hung loosely off my shoulders. I sat down on the cot and stared at the floor. The uniform did not make me feel like part of the German army. It made me feel like I was still just a boy, not ready for war.

I stretched out on the cot but knew I would not sleep a wink. Let me just say that the ceiling was white with peeling paint. Everyone around me was snoring. Everyone around me was tougher. If I believed in God, I would have prayed. Instead, I lay like a dummy. At the first glimmer of sunrise, I sneaked out of my bed and peered out the window. Rolf patrolled a large exercise area that was surrounded by a wire fence. I realized that Rolf was no longer a puppy, but a full-grown German shepherd with classic brown and black fur, built like a wolf with erect ears and a long slender muzzle. Sometimes I wondered what went through his head. I knew that he could not think in terms of words, but instincts stirred inside him, anxious about my whereabouts. Metelmann walked up to the fence. Rolf drew back his ears and snarled. Metelmann took a chain and slammed it against the fence. Rolf barked loudly in retort. Anxious to get to the kennels, I shined my shoes, made my cot, and stood at attention, ready for inspection. There were twelve soldiers in our barracks. We did not talk or look at each other. Metelmann scrutinized us up and down.

"Dismissed," he said and saluted. "Heil Hitler."

Rolf was so excited to see me that he peed on the concrete floor. I opened the kennel door, and he burst out of the gate, knocking me over. He sniffed my uniform from cuff to collar. Already, he was doing his job. I looped the required spike collar over his neck and gripped the leather leash. We reported for our first lesson. The training class was a vacant building with no windows. Herbert Metelmann awaited us. Rolf sat with ears perked. Sometimes it really seemed like he understood the German language.

Metelmann began, "The dog must learn the importance of a wounded man. That is his principle business in life. News of the wounded must be brought to his master. He must not bark, because the enemy shoots dogs on sight. Now, I have a special strap."

Rolf practically inhaled the strap, absorbing every particle of scent. Metelmann buckled the strap into his dog collar.

"At night, he will scout the battlefield looking for injured soldiers. If no wounded soldier is found, he trots back and lies down. If he finds a wounded soldier, he grasps the strap in his mouth and returns. This shows that there is a German soldier out there who is alive. Then he leads you back to the wounded man. Each dog carries a first aid package strapped on his back. When the wounded are found, the soldier may take the package. Rolf will also be taught to carry letters from post to post. Dogs have many uses in war. Russians strap explosives to suicide dogs and send them out to blow up tanks. It is an effective tactic."

Thus, began our career in the army. One morning into it, life was not so bad. I began to feel almost optimistic. Rolf picked up obedience training quickly, learned to heel, to sit on command, to lie down, and to retrieve. Rolf was taught to be silent. I trained Rolf to travel quietly, to avoid higher land, and to cover open spaces on the run. For this aspect of the training, I was relieved to be out of the vacant building and into fields near the barracks.

"Now," said Metelmann. "Take off the spike collar. Make the dog sit down. Drop the leash."

Rolf lay flat on the floor, his bright eyes looking up with trust. That expression broke my fantasy of army life. For a brief moment, I pictured Rolf dead in a foxhole, covered with blood. Rolf inched toward me, whimpering.

"Your dog is in a down. Tell him to stay," Metelmann ordered.

I gestured 'down' with my hands. Rolf went flat.

"Now put your hand in his mouth. Keep it there for 30 seconds and then command 'retrieve.' Wait briefly then command 'out.' This will teach him to carry the strap gently in his mouth to tell us he has found a wounded soldier.

Remember to praise him."

Rolf was a star student, breezing through training. He learned to hunt for objects that were thrown in the grass or hidden in the mess hall or even buried in fields. As training progressed, I tied cloth to a string and dragged it through acres of field and then hid the object.

"Retrieve!" I commanded.

No longer a puppy with big clumsy paws, he was now a muscular young dog. Rolf bolted into the field, straight to the hidden object. He trotted back proudly, wagging his tail. It was almost like old times, rubbing his soft ears and feeling him lick my hand. For a fleeting second, I forgot about Hans and war. "Good boy," I said and wrapped my arms around his furry neck. On graduation day, Rolf was fitted with first-aid bags that slung across his body. Metelmann slid a Red Cross band on my sleeve and pulled papers from a leather satchel. Part of me knew what he was about to say. The rest of me did not want to hear.

Metelmann spoke in a crisp voice, "You are going to the Russian front. Look for a medic in charge of the first-aid tent. He will tell you what to do. I have been notified by high command that metal for dog cages is in short supply. Dogs must be kept with their trainers at all times. They will not be kept in kennels. Hand this official letter to your supervising officer. Heil Hitler."

Winter raged on in Russia. I wiggled my fingers and wondered if they would freeze solid. Frostbite was a terrible thing. Fingers broke off like icicles from a roof. I rubbed my hands on Rolf's warm fur. "Come on, Rolf, time to pack."

Chapter 7

Officer Goldmann

March,1943 - frozen plains of southern Russia

Officer Karl Goldmann, my leader on the battlefield, was the tallest man in the world. When he stood in the midst of a hundred men, he towered over them all. He was built like an aspen tree in height and strength. His face was a long oval punctuated by round glasses. Fixed to the side of his head were large ears that scooped out almost like small cups. With hair light brown and wavy, he struck a radical contrast to the stiff black hair of Adolph Hitler. It is difficult to describe his eyes. I would call them hazel with mixtures of olive and brown. Complex, they were, with a depth that radiated intelligence. Add to this description a confusing twist. He wore an SS Waffen Nazi uniform, representing the most dreaded agency in Nazi Germany. The SS was charged with security, surveillance, and combat. He wore a field gray uniform with a patch that displayed a lightning bolt logo. All those who wore this patch were expected to fight to the death for Adolph Hitler. Here was a man to hate.

The first words I heard him say were to another soldier, "Hold my glasses." You see, he was about to step into a serious fistfight with an enlisted man named Herbert. Evidently, trouble had been brewing for weeks between the two men, so a crowd quickly formed around the combatants. Herbert had a crooked nose, like that of a punch-drunk boxer. Surely, the lanky Goldmann would go down quickly.

"Stop your harassment or you will regret you ever met me," Goldmann said.

"I already regret knowing you. I will beat you to a pulp," he replied.

"Look, soldier, I've asked you to stop."

Herbert sucked in a large amount of saliva and spat into Goldmann's face. There was no turning back now. After wiping spit from his face, Goldmann slipped a small black book into his jacket. Herbert and Goldmann circled each other with fists up, like professional boxers. Herbert unleashed a quick jab toward his opponent's stomach. That foray was easily blocked. In a flash, Goldmann grabbed Herbert's arms and twisted them behind his back.

"Better stop now," Goldmann said.

At that, Herbert tried to head butt the officer, but the blow fell below its mark, hitting Goldmann's chest. That was a bad choice by Herbert. In rapid succession, Goldmann pushed him away and launched a resounding punch to Herbert's face. The man went down like a chopped tree and lay bleeding at

Goldmann's feet. This incident was a perplexing introduction to the dynamics of war. One thing I knew, German soldiers fought the enemy, not each other, and superior officers do not fight enlisted men. This fight was a major violation. Over the next few days, word spread quickly to the higher command at camp, then to superiors in Berlin, then back to camp. It took only two days for orders to come from Berlin. At roll call, Goldmann was stripped of his elite status as an SS officer. Without the slightest wince, Goldmann handed over his SS jacket and donned the humble brown uniform of a field medic. On his sleeve was a Red Cross armband, just like mine. He saluted and immediately went to a jeep where a driver sat waiting for him.

I could not take my eyes off this tall medic. He chatted briefly to the driver who nodded in a sympathetic manner. Rolf looked up at me with a quizzical expression, probably wondering why we stood there doing nothing. A persistent feeling came over me, a feeling that stayed with me the entire war. *Follow that man and you will return home.* That was the thought. It was vague and not much on which to pin my survival but gave me hope. Here is when I felt a gentle nudge that came from…someone…somewhere. I attempted to dismiss it but found myself walking toward the jeep with a tiny bit of hope.

"Felix Culpa Schmidt, reporting for duty, sir," I attempted to sound confident.

"Welcome to the Russian winter. Our company has been in need of a casualty dog. Men are freezing to death out on the battlefield before we can reach them. I will take you to the hospital tent." Goldmann gazed up at the sky. "Dark clouds are gathering. It looks like another blizzard is coming."

Bitter winds blew across the Russian plains, stinging my cheeks. Air puffed out of my mouth like steam. Night came upon us, and with it, came snow squalls, whirling and whipping, grinding away the world into emptiness. Imagine, my confused mind said to me, you could take one step and walk off the end of the earth. An icy gust slapped me in the face, shaking me back to reality in the furry form of a brown and black friend. Rolf pranced next to me and looked up with mischievous eyes. I crouched down to hug him. "You want to play! What a crazy dog." Rolf yanked on the long leather leash as we broke into a trot. Inside the tent were rows of injured men lying on cots. Our only source of light was one oil lamp that sat on a medicine table near two empty cots. Goldmann handed me a pile of neatly folded wool blankets. They were battle-worn blankets with moth holes and ragged edges. A blast of wind shook the tent like sails of a ship. Snow beat against the canvas. My nose stung with cold.

Methodically, Goldmann checked the men, and I handed him blankets for the injured.

"No one is in danger of dying. With this blizzard, there is nothing more we can do. That is your cot. Try to get some sleep. The Russians usually attack after a storm." He blew out the lamp.

It was so black that I wondered if my eyes were really open. Fierce winds beat against the tent. I patted my stomach as a sign to Rolf. Without hesitation, Rolf jumped on top of me. Under his thick winter coat, I grew drowsy and fell asleep with his warm breath on my cheek. My slumber was broken by the sound of a man's voice. Goldmann was talking in his sleep. I lifted my head to hear. He said, "A briefcase...in July." They seemed like harmless words to me, but not to Goldmann. By the way he yelped, I guessed he was having a nightmare. The words bounced around in my head but made no sense. I rested on my back and stared into the night, waiting for dawn and the start of my first day on the battlefield. I tried to calculate my chances of survival.

Chapter 8

Ghost Dog

The next morning, I pulled aside the tent flap to the sight of our camp transfigured by drifts. The sun shone through a dazzling snow mist. I felt wrapped in a world of blue sky and snow. Rolf and I ventured out, awaiting orders. All around, men were busy shoveling, cleaning rifles, and setting up machine gun nests. The enemy was hidden behind low hills to the east.

"You, soldier, take sentry duty behind those sandbags. Take the dog with you," ordered an officer.

As I stared out over snow-covered plains, my eyes began to water. Ridges formed a line to my right and ahead were small hills. On this horizon, I spotted an object of unknown origin floating above the horizon. Rolf's ears twitched with energy. I perched my elbows on sandbags and peered through binoculars. At first, the image was blurry, but with some adjustment of the focusing ring, the object became clear. It was a white German shepherd, silent and motionless, in the posture of a bird dog pointing at prey. After several minutes, he crept toward the ridge. Through a wavy mirage on the horizon, a Russian infantry battalion moved toward us in a straight line. I thought for sure we were about to be slaughtered. Suddenly, a blaze of bullets came from the ridge, fired by highly-trained marksmen. I surmised that white dog was a scout dog who had alerted the Russians of German snipers hidden in the grove. Russians fell like dominoes, one after another. A second line of Russians sent a round of ammunition at the snipers. Unexpectedly, the Russians drew back. It could be a trick to lure us into the open.

"Some of our men may be hurt. Send out the dog," an officer said.

Two months of training had prepared us for this moment. "Go find!" I yelled. Rolf took off like a bullet, straight to the ridge. He looked like an easy target: brown fur against white snow. If one injured Russian picked up his rifle, Rolf would be a goner. With powerful strides, he plowed through deep snow and disappeared over the ridge. Minutes seemed like hours as I waited for some sign of life. In a burst of snow, he ran out of the grove straight for me. I focused the binoculars on him. Sure enough, he had the strap in his mouth. Rolf barreled toward me and leaped over the sandbags in triumph. I glanced out at the hills. No Russians. Or were there? I hesitated.

At that moment, Goldmann appeared next to me, carrying a

Red Cross backpack. "Do whatever I do. Keep your head down." Reality descended on me. I was now under full command of a violent man with a quick temper. One slight misstep on my part and he could beat me to a bloody pulp. As a soldier in the German army, I had no choice but to obey, otherwise I could be shot for treason. "Our machine guns will cover us. Now give your command to the dog." That I did.

Energized by a sense of mission, Rolf leaped into action. Goldmann dragged a stretcher onto the battlefield. At any instant, a Russian soldier could shoot us down. I imagined myself shot in the chest, blood oozing onto the snow. Gusts of wind blew powdery snow all around us. This provided additional cover. We forged ahead and made it safely over drifts. Six soldiers used snow mounds as perches for their rifles. They squinted through scopes, eyes riveted to the horizon. Rolf led us to an embankment, slightly removed from the other men. I searched and saw no injured man; it looked like Rolf had failed on his first assignment, yet he did not act that way. He was still on mission, sniffing snow drifts. Almost imperceptibly, I saw a drift stir. Rolf buried his nose into the mound. Goldmann followed his lead and lightly brushed away snow. Buried in the drift was a soldier. At first sight, the man looked like a frozen corpse. He blinked, and snow fell from his eyelashes.

Quickly, Goldmann examined the wound and discovered a bullet in the arm. Goldmann tore away the sleeve, and tied a tourniquet to the upper arm. The soldier's arm looked like raw red meat; blood spurted out of an artery. The bullet was imbedded just below a flap of skin. Snow began to fall. Goldmann whipped tweezers from the first-aid bag. With his nose almost in the wound, he pinched tweezers and gently pulled out the bullet. Within minutes, Goldmann cleaned the wound, applied iodine, and wrapped it with thick layers of gauze. Gently, we lifted the soldier onto our stretcher. Snow fell like buzzing bees all around us, blinding me. It was impossible to know which way to go. Rolf took the lead and plowed through blizzard conditions. All we could do was trust in his nose. He paused and sniffed the wind—this way. He leaped forward. I saw black shapes ahead. We were mere shadows walking straight into our own machine gun nests. They could mistake us for the enemy and mow us down.

"Red Cross!" Goldmann shouted into the gale. I saw a shape stand up and motion. They did not shoot. With renewed energy, we pressed forward through drifts and into the safety of camp. Two soldiers lifted the stretcher and carried the injured man into the hospital tent. Numbness set into my fingers and toes. We followed them into the tent. As I shook snow from my jacket, Goldmann set a tub of warm water in front of me, unlaced my boots, and examined my toes. Circulation had been cut off and now my toes were white.

"First sign of frostbite. We will slowly warm them," Goldmann said. So I sat with my pants rolled up and feet in a bucket of warm water. Goldmann sat with me.

"Do you know what day it is?" he asked. I did not know.

"It is Ash Wednesday," he said and wiped dripping snow from his face. Solemnly, he pulled from his pocket that small black book. It was a Christian prayer book. As he made the sign of the cross, I noticed that his fingertips had turned white. This did not seem to matter to him. I was in no mood to pray. On this frigid Russian plain, God was farther away from me than ever before. Goldmann continued to pray. Still, this did not gain my trust. Quite the opposite. This man was a hypocrite. One day he beat up a fellow soldier, and the next day he prayed. Since my feet were stuck in a bucket of water, I was stuck listening to him. Yet, my hard heart could not change certain things. This certain thing was that his voice sounded remarkably like Father Mueller.

Chapter 9

War Machine

The season of Lent did not begin with the peal of church bells. It began with the roar of artillery from that eastern hill where enemy soldiers lay hidden. We responded with machine gun fire. German tanks rolled into battle. Infantry men followed. Swift movement caught my eye. It was an animal running at the tanks. Through binoculars, I saw a brown dog with packs strapped on his back. He lay flat in front of a tank as it rolled over him. Upon impact, the tank exploded. Metal flew high into the air amid red flames and a black cloud of smoke. The infantry fell flat on frozen ground. Goldmann stood next to me, staring into his binoculars. Lines of Russian soldiers flooded over the hill. Rifle fire split the air in loud cracks. We responded with machine gun fire. More German tanks rolled forward, mowing down Russians. On the crest of the hill, our tanks stopped. We had gained ground in this bloody march to circle Moscow and fly the Nazi flag over their capital. This would demoralize our enemy to the point of surrender. That hope flickered in my heart. Soon the war would be over, and I could go home. All was quiet.

Goldmann motioned to me. "Send the dog."

I gave the command. "Go find." Rolf bounded down onto the battlefield, toward fallen soldiers a short distance away. Efficiently, he sniffed uniforms in search of the living. Many must have been dead. He stopped abruptly. Despite a withering barrage of bullets, one soldier had survived. Rolf scooped the strap into his mouth and raced back to us. Goldmann hoisted his first-aid bag and we followed Rolf. Many soldiers lay dead around us, blood seeping out of open wounds. Dead men stared up at a tranquil blue sky. Rolf led us to a survivor. The front of his uniform was darkened with blood. Goldmann unbuttoned the soldier's jacket to reveal a deep wound in the abdomen; blood spilled onto the snow. Goldmann applied pressure with thick gauze but could not stem the flow. The soldier mumbled incoherently. Goldmann leaned closer.

"In your pocket?" Goldmann asked. It was a letter stating his last request, sealed with a wax cross. On the eastern hill, the white scout dog appeared. Rolf growled, a rumbling that rose from deep in his throat. I held my hand flat against his nose, the command for silence. Suddenly, the scout stiffened and pointed. Goldmann saw the dog's signal.

"The enemy is advancing. Back to camp. Quickly." he said. With our lives at stake, deep drifts blocked our passage, but we plowed forward. "Red Cross," Goldmann yelled into fierce winds. "Red Cross. Hold your fire!" He knew that German artillery could mistake us for enemy troops. With each breath of frigid air, my lungs ached, my legs buckled, but I stayed upright and kept my head down. Closer we came to camp, hidden by blowing snow. "Red Cross!" In one life-saving moment, someone heard, and the shooting stopped. We crawled over sandbags to safety, to an encampment preparing for onslaught from Russian soldiers who never cried retreat.

"How close are they?" It was the voice of a radio operator listening to a small, rectangular field radio with plug-in holes and two radio dials—one for frequency and the other for volume. He inserted plugs from his headphones and held them up to his ear. It was picking up messages from a German armored tank out in the battlefield.

As he listened, his eyes narrowed. "I hear gunfire. Are you under attack?" He clapped the headphones tighter to his ears. "You see a Russian dog running toward you?"

He waited for an answer. An explosion shook the ground. Great billows of black smoke blew over us. The camp radio operator adjusted his headphones and rapidly turned dials. Dejectedly, he took off the headphones. Wild gusts whipped across the plain. Another storm beat down on us. Temperatures plummeted. The Russian army stopped their advance, for that moment in this place, allowing us to spend the night in our tents. Huddled in an army tent and cut off from the outside world, I did not know about the Battle of Stalingrad, but learned later that the German 6th army engaged in fierce hand-to-hand combat with the Russians. German planes bombed Stalingrad and reduced the city to rubble. Many civilians were killed. More than two million soldiers fought in the Battle of Stalingrad; more than 300,000 Germans were killed. It was the largest, bloodiest battle in the history of warfare. The German 6th army was trapped in Stalingrad. On February 2, 1943, the German 6th army stopped their siege of Russia. Orders came from central command to pull our troops out of the Russian plains and await reassignment.

It was the beginning of the end for Hitler's army.

Chapter 10

Invasion

Italy, 1943

Once again, we were put on a train, Rolf by my side and Goldmann across the aisle studying an Italian grammar book. Our destination was the island of Sicily, off the coast of Italy. Allied forces were on a relentless offensive, determined to trap Germans in southern Italy. Our mission was to set up a line of defense to protect German troops as they retreated to continental Italy. Rolf put his chin on my lap and sighed. I tapped his nose with a letter from home. As Papa predicted, the envelope was torn open.

It read, *we try to keep life on the farm going on as normal, but it is not the same without you. We do our daily chores and pray that your guardian angel watches over you. Foxes are on the prowl. They tried to break into the chicken coop, but they could not get through the wire fence. Write when you can. Love, Papa.*

I remembered the code. Gestapo soldiers were searching houses for infractions. .... *they could not get through the wire fence.* That meant they burst into our house, searched closets, under beds, in the barn, but found nothing. I wiped moisture off the train window and watched farmhouses, pastures, woods speed by–reminders of home. It seemed possible that neighbors told the Gestapo about Willy. Neighbor betrayed neighbor. Father Mueller anticipated this betrayal. Father Mueller saved Willy's life. This thought sank into my heart like a pebble in a deep pond. *Follow that man and you will return home.* A tiny flame of hope could not be snuffed out.

It was time to rest. Rolf was asleep with his head on my lap, already dreaming. His eyes rolled wildly in collaboration with his wiggly paws. I think he was dreaming about running through wheat fields back home. I sighed and looked across the aisle at Goldmann. He was reading that black prayer book with intensity. He lifted his head and spoke softly, not realizing that I could hear him.

He said, "Please Lord, I beg of you, give me courage. I will deliver the message, but I don't know how. Protect me." I pulled my hat down, pretending to sleep. Goldmann must be keeping a dark secret that preyed on his mind, seeping out in sleep talking and now, in this prayer. Is he involved in some kind of plot? My mind was too full to think anymore. I turned and saw my reflection in the window. I wore a gray Panzer army wool field hat with a visor and two buttons in the front. Tension lines gathered around the corner of my eyes. I bit my bottom lip, causing a dark spot to form below my mouth. My eyelids drooped, heavy with fatigue. Rolf snuggled closer to me and I fell asleep.

Our train pulled slowly into the station in Munich. An announcement came over the speaker; *Passengers are allowed to leave the train for a ten-minute stop.* That was a relief. Rolf and I stepped onto the platform and heard the drone of an airplane. It was a British bomber swooping in a curve just above the treetops. A door opened up in the belly of the plane and thousands of papers fluttered down. One leaflet landed in a puddle next to my foot. I looked around to be sure nobody saw me. I picked up the paper. It was from the White Rose. Water dripped off the edges as I read,

Fellow Fighters in the Resistance!

Shaken and broken, our people behold the loss of the men of Stalingrad. Three hundred and thirty thousand German men have been senselessly and irresponsibly driven to death and destruction by the inspired strategy of our World War I Private First Class, Fuhrer, we thank you...The day of reckoning has come, the reckoning of German youth with the most abominable tyrant our people have ever been forced to endure. In the name of German youth, we demand restitution by Adolph Hitler's state of our personal freedom, that most precious treasure that we have.

I knew this was the voice of Hans Scholl. Tears blurred my eyes as I read on,

The frightful bloodbath has opened the eyes of even the stupidest German…The German people look to us to break the National socialist terror through the power of the spirit…Our people stand ready to rebel…in a fervent new breakthrough of freedom and honor.

I swallowed hard, trying to suppress the screaming that took place inside me. Rolf jumped up and put his paws on my shoulders. He gazed at me like I was the bravest soldier in the world. He studied my face intently.

"You know what is going on inside me," I said. Rolf put his nose to my nose. I pulled out the Hitler Youth patch and squeezed it in a tight fist. "If I get home alive, I will always speak up for what is good and true and noble. I will never betray Hans Scholl again. I make this solemn oath, even if it means that I must die. Do you hear me, Rolf?" my faithful companion cocked his head and whimpered, like he understood completely. We climbed back on the train.

For many days, we traveled the length of Italy, past towering mountains of rock and glaciers, deep valleys, and forests of oak and chestnut trees. Ever south we journeyed, gathered provisions and then marched on foot to the tip of Italy. Military crafts brought us across the Straits of Messina to the northeast coast of Sicily.

We staked out our position above a small village located at the edge of the Tyrrhenian Sea. Steep cliffs and small valleys created ideal terrain for machine guns. This was fortunate because we had no heavy weapons, no cannons, and no extra ammunition. Rolf and I lay flat and looked down at a dirt road curving through the countryside. A vehicle headed our way. I aimed my binoculars. It was an olive-green jeep with four seats and a large Red Cross painted on the back. The driver was a stocky man with a round face. He waved a white handkerchief and climbed toward us.

"Welcome to the 9th German Panzer Division. My name is Baden, your driver. We have been without a medic for three weeks. Our last medic was killed in action," he said. "I see that you brought a dog. Is he a sentry dog?"

"He works with the medical corps and is trained to find injured German soldiers. When was the last attack?" Goldmann asked.

"Two days ago. We lost fifty men, only 120 of us left. We are also down to one homing pigeon. All the other birds have been shot down. Private Johann Inkling is in charge of our birds. We call him Private Pigeon Man," Baden said.

As I turned to find water for Rolf, I heard cooing from behind rocks. Rolf investigated, and I followed. We found a young soldier – perhaps twenty years old—opening a bird cage. Private Inkling was short, with black curly hair, and a stubbly beard. I rubbed the peach fuzz on my chin. *Someday, maybe*, I thought. He carried a shoulder bag filled with corn and seed. A leather gun case was strapped to his belt.

"It sounds like you are an expert in training birds. My name is Felix," I said awkwardly and then pointed to the case. "Is there a gun in there?"

"Well, I sure don't carry daisies." He unsnapped the flap and produced a German Luger sidearm with rigid barrel.

"Where did you get it?" I asked.

"Off a dead German officer."

"Ever discharge it?"

"Not yet. I am waiting for just the right time, two bullets ready to go. Back home, I used to shoot squirrels: a crack shot, you might say." He slid it back into the case.

Just to break the ice, I started to talk about my war experience, hoping to impress him, "We just arrived. Our medic unit just came down from the Russian front. Sergeant Karl Goldmann is my supervisor. Blizzards blew across the Russian plain. Temperatures dropped to 50 below. I got frost bite on my feet. Do you know the Russians have suicide dogs? They strap explosives on them and the dogs blow up tanks and themselves. Horrible."

Johann said nothing to me, but cooed back at the pigeon, sprinkling seeds in small metal trays. Gently, he stroked the head of a black bird with bright red eyes and then pointed to a small bell hanging from the cage. Obediently, the bird rang the bell.

"Smart bird," I said.

He looked suspiciously at Rolf. "Does that dog eat birds?" Johann asked sharply.

"Not lately," I said. Rolf had been known to eat chickens back at our farm. At this inopportune moment, Rolf licked his chops.

"He better not or I will personally drown him in the Tyrrhenian Sea."

It seemed wise to ignore this comment and push on with the conversation. "This is Rolf. He is a highly-trained Red Cross dog. Rolf has saved many soldiers out on the battlefield. Isn't that right, my friend?" Rolf ignored me. For the moment, he sniffed the cage. Feathers tickled his nose, making him sneeze. The pigeon hopped around his cage, ruffling feathers and squawking. I decided it prudent to keep Rolf away. My best bet was to entice him with water. After swirling the water pan under his nose, I placed the pan down. Rolf lapped it up eagerly. Dogs were not a good topic, so I changed subjects.

"My grandfather trained pigeons in The Great War," I said. "He never talked about it. He never talked about war. The Great War was supposed to be the war to end all wars."

"I guess they were wrong," Johann said.

"Yes, I guess they were wrong."

Johann looked over at me. "I never imagined myself to be a soldier. Yet, here I am, Private Pigeon Man reporting for duty. Sometimes I think I like pigeons better than people. I call my bird Thunderbolt, Bolt for short." At that point a soldier ran toward us. He handed Johann a small slip of paper which he rolled up and stuffed it in a canister. Gently, he cradled Bolt and clamped the container on his leg. He tossed the bird up in the air and it took off. I had never seen a bird fly so fast or so high.

"Where is he going? I asked.

"He is flying back to Rome headquarters. That is his home base. I trained him there and then he was dropped by crate from a bomber to this location. There is a parachute attached to the crate. Whenever we have to let headquarters know about enemy positions, we send Bolt. Some messages are too sensitive to report on a radio, so we use pigeons. Allied forces can intercept radio messages. When Bolt returns, he rings the bell." Johann looked up at the black feathery dot disappear into a cloud.

"Sometimes I worry that he won't come back. All our pigeons have either been shot down or attacked by buzzards," he said, still staring into clouds. "Sometimes I worry that I won't make it home. Do you?"

"All the time," I said.

"I did not expect to be drafted. My life seemed to be going in quite another direction. I was studying..." Johann began but stopped.

"Studying what?" I asked.

"Philosophy, theology and the like..." his voice trailed off.

"Oh," I said.

As the sun set, it was time for supper. Our camp cook lit a small outdoor stove designed to conceal smoke from Allied artillery. Greasy green pea soup bubbled in a pot, thick with sliced carrots and a chunk of pork fat that floated on top. Our ration included one slice of bread. We filled our metal mess kits and sat on rocks. Johann and I sat next to each other and ate in silence. Cautiously, Rolf nuzzled Private Pigeon Man. Sometimes it seemed that Rolf understood people better than I did. To my surprise, Johann did not brush off the chicken-eating dog. Maybe Johann and I could be friends after all.

Chapter 11

Threats

For two days, Johann barely spoke to me. He spent many hours scanning the sky in search of Bolt. Puffy white clouds appeared, and buzzards glided effortlessly over our heads. A missing bird was the least of our worries for now. Allied airplanes droned overhead. They flew out of a cloud bank over sparkling seas. Goldmann raised his binoculars. "Reconnaissance. They are gathering intelligence for an attack. Go hide in the cliffs."

Our battalion fled for cover. Rolf and I hid in the shade of a rocky ledge. Johann lay flat next to us and pulled his helmet down tightly to protect his face. At that instant, he pulled something out of his pocket and gripped it tightly. I could see him clutch black rosary beads and he whispered familiar words, "Hail Mary full of grace..." My heart pounded. My tongue felt pasty and dry. I could neither think nor pray. Planes flew so low, I could see U.S. flags emblazoned on the tails. They dipped even lowered. The roar of engines rang in my ears. As the pilots looked down from their cockpits, we must have looked like ants. Goldmann looked unfazed by this show of power. Six battleships plowed through the sea, straight for us, with giant cannons aimed at our location. With bursts of white smoke, missiles soared in our direction. They hurtled overhead with wild screams. Cliffs exploded all around us. Men flew into the air like rag dolls.

"We will set up a first-aid station under those cliffs. Keep your head down," Goldmann said. Movement was made difficult as we crept through vines and thorn bushes toward cliffs just below us. I crawled into the shade of a long overhang that hid us from the enemy. Rolf crouched, waiting for a command.

"When enemy fire stops, send him," Goldmann ordered.

Helpless, I watched in horror as U.S. Navy destroyers launched missile after missile in a systematic attack. Black smoke curled and formed clouds above the treetops. Explosions blew craters in the landscape. German soldiers, one second crawling on their bellies toward cover, and in the next second, vaporized in a bomb blast. I felt overcome with scorching thirst. When the bombardment stopped, my ears buzzed, my bones ached. Sounds of war vibrated through my body.

"Go find!" I gestured to Rolf.

Many minutes passed before Rolf returned with a strap in his mouth, his fur splattered with human blood. Despite the carnage, he had found a soldier with a flicker of life in him. Goldmann added rolls of gauze to his first-aid kit and moved toward the battlefield. Rolf led us past dead soldiers to a man lying behind a boulder. We gently placed him on a stretcher and carried him back to the first aid shelter. It was a grave injury to his hand. "There has been much loss of blood," Goldmann said. He tied a tourniquet tightly around the arm. As I watched a red puddle of blood form in the dirt, the Red Cross jeep pulled up next to us. Baden jumped out and squatted next to Goldmann.

"You must save the dying," Baden said.

"I don't understand what you mean. Look at my hands covered in blood. What more can I do?" Goldmann replied with exasperation.

"Goldmann, listen. It is their souls that we must save. They die without Holy Communion. You need to go back to the village and find a priest."

Now, this was a strange request from an ambulance driver to an army medic. Only priests could distribute communion and every priest must have fled the village. I peered out at the Tyrrhenian Sea. Navy battleships still had us in their crosshairs. To hand out wafers of bread in such times of peril was an absurd idea.

Goldmann hesitated. "I must not leave the battlefield."

"If you were dying on these cliffs, what would be your final request?" Baden asked.

"I would want to look in the face of a priest and receive my last Holy Communion."

"When war broke out, you were studying in a Franciscan seminary. You told me about a fistfight you had to defend the Faith. A soldier saw you reading your black prayer book and ridiculed you. God has called you to save souls."

I stared at this man in a uniform of the German army. I could not imagine Karl Goldmann in the brown robes of a Franciscan friar. I could not picture him saying Mass. He was a soldier, not a priest. Goldmann stood up and watched the sun setting over the gray towers of battleships. We were surrounded by the enemy and low on ammunition. No priest in his right mind would expose himself to these dangers.

"Our commander will not give permission for me to go into the village," Goldmann said.

Baden spoke with urgency. "We need surgical supplies. Use that as an excuse."

That is what we did. Since I was under orders to stay with my assigned medic, Rolf and I climbed into the backseat of the jeep and we headed to the village of Patti. It was a ghost town. All inhabitants had fled when they saw us set up machine guns on the cliffs. The only signs of life were escaped chickens foraging in the grass. To them, life was still normal and bugs plentiful. Baden slowed to a halt and drove to the edge of town. Just ahead was a small stone chapel nestled in a grove of olive trees. In the yard were flowering bushes filled with bumble bees. Goldmann pulled on the heavy wooden door. As we entered the dark church, I felt a surge in my heart. *He is here.* Both soldiers knelt. I did too. I watched these two men in Nazi uniforms, splattered with blood, pray before the crucifix. It was not a long period of prayer, for we knew the enemy would begin another attack at any time. We rose and went in search of a priest. This seemed like an impossible task. Surely, any priest fled along with the villagers.

Behind the chapel was a humble house surrounded by grape arbors. At the entrance was a vine-covered trellis laden with purple grapes. Goldmann knocked on the door. A stout priest in brown robes opened the door. He stepped back in horror at the sight of German soldiers. Goldmann took off his hat and bowed respectfully.

"I am sorry to disturb you, but we have an urgent need. I am a medic with the 29th German Panzer division. I serve soldiers on the battlefield. Many are dying without Holy Communion. I need a priest to bring them the Blessed Sacrament," he said.

"That is impossible. You must get permission from our bishop. He lives in the cathedral at the top of that hill a few miles west of here," he replied.

"Please, Father, won't you come with me? There is no time to waste. Men are dying, even as we speak."

The old priest shook his head and gestured toward the door. There was no arguing with him. Off we rode up a winding path to the cathedral. Far below, I could see two armies dug into their positions. For the time being, all was quiet. In front of the cathedral was a square with a marble pool containing cool water. I took off my helmet and scooped water for Rolf. Meanwhile, Goldman and Baden knocked on the church door. No answer. Rolf pulled on the leash in the direction of a gated flower garden. We went through the gate. A solitary priest sat on a bench, reading his prayer book. He was thin with a long black beard and dirty cassock. Our sudden appearance startled him.

"Nazis are not welcome here. You must leave immediately," he said.

It was not my custom to contradict an adult, but I mustered up courage. "My superior wishes to speak to you about an urgent matter."

"I do not care to hear your request. Now leave."

"But, Father..."

The garden gate creaked and Goldmann stepped forward. "I am sorry to disturb you, but I need to speak to the bishop."

"Why do you need to speak to the bishop?"

Irritation crept into Goldmann's voice. "I do not wish to speak to you, Father. I must speak to the bishop."

Now the priest sounded mad. "You can tell me your business. I am the bishop."

"We have no time for jokes. Lead me to the bishop."

"And I have no time for your insolence. I am Bishop Morelli," and on that note, the priest reached into his pocket to reveal a gold ring worn only by bishops. He put it on his finger and held it out to Goldmann.

"I beg your forgiveness, Bishop Morelli..." he said and knelt to kiss the ring.

"What is your business?" the bishop asked tersely.

"Before the war began, I studied in a Franciscan seminary in Germany. Against our wills, seminarians were drafted into the German army. Now I am a medic out on the battlefield. Many soldiers are dying without the sacraments. Their souls are in grave danger."

"That is the duty of your chaplain."

"We have no chaplain."

"That is no concern of mine. I cannot help you."

"Bishop, I do have a request. Please assign a priest to bring Holy Communion to the injured and dying."

"Send one of my priests in the line of fire? That is out of the question. We have nothing more to discuss. Now leave," the bishop turned his back on us and headed toward the garden gate.

"I beg of you, please send a priest. It is a matter of heaven or hell for these soldiers."

The bishop spun toward us, "Absolutely not! I will not endanger the life of my priests to serve German soldiers. Germans are not liked here!"

Now Goldmann began to yell, "It is not a matter of Germans or Italians! It is a matter of Catholics dying without the sacraments! Have you ever heard soldiers moaning in agony? For the last time, Your Excellency, please send me a priest."

"No. Never."

"I am sorry to say that now you leave me no choice," Goldmann said. In one smooth motion, he unsnapped the flap over his gun and stepped toward the bishop. He held the pistol under the bishop's nose. Sweat beaded up on the bishop's forehead. At first, he appeared frozen in fear, unable to speak.

"Lower the gun and I will give you an answer," the bishop said.

Goldmann stepped back, but kept the gun pointed at him.

Bishop Morelli said, "I have a document from the Vatican that permits me to give you the Blessed Sacrament. Follow me."

He led us to his office and sat at his desk, quickly writing these words:

The Bishop's Residence

     Patti 4.8.43

In view of the extraordinary conditions and the special faculties granted by the Holy See, we grant the Catholic cleric of the 29th German Panzer Division to bring with due reverence Holy Communion to his comrades, especially the wounded.

Signed + Salvatore Morelli

As the bishop handed over the paper, Allied bombers roared overhead. More German soldiers would soon be dying. We hurried to the tabernacle. Bishop Morelli placed ten consecrated Hosts in a gold pyx which Goldmann placed safely in a pocket over his heart.

Chapter 12

Mission of Death

Back at camp, a motorcycle sped to us in a cloud of dust. It skidded to a halt and the driver looked up from the controls, his face covered in dirt. When he took off his goggles, clean circles remained around his eyes.

"Bombs exploded in the middle of our battalion," he said breathlessly. "Men are dying without medical help."

"Where are they?" Goldmann asked.

He gestured toward the village. "You have to cross main street and over that bridge."

Sometimes it is wise not to think. We had no time to think of that open street with no cover where British soldiers guard every inch. The bridge also was surrounded by British soldiers. In war, a soldier keeps moving, like a machine, not thinking that each step could be his last.

Goldmann stared at me. "I need you and your dog to find men quickly. It is a dangerous mission. Can you do this?"

Machine me did not think. Machine me said yes. Baden revved the engine. Rolf hopped in the backseat. I sat on the leather seat, already covered with muddy paw prints and dog hair. Baden stepped on the gas. Goldmann held up the Red Cross flag. We sped along a mountain road with sharp curves and steep cliffs. Baden gripped the steering wheel as we swerved on the narrow road. Rolf quivered with excitement. I held him close and felt his steady breathing. Machine guns opened fire on us. I fell to the floor and covered my head. Rolf lay flat on the floor. Goldmann sat upright in his seat, waving the flag. As bullets blasted into the rock ledge, stones rained down on us. At any instant, I expected to see Goldmann slump into a bloody heap, but he held position until the shooting ceased. Sounds of our engine echoed through the valley. Baden accelerated toward the village. He skidded to a stop behind rock walls that lined the shore near a bridge arching a river. On the other side was a farmhouse. Rolf sniffed the air and growled. I followed his gaze to a thicket across the river. Sun glinted off metal surfaces. I squinted and saw machine guns aimed at the bridge.

I tugged on Goldmann's shirt. "Sir, machine guns have position across the river."

"Where?"

I pointed to the thicket.

"We still have to cross. Wounded men lay dying in that farmhouse."

"But, sir..."

Goldmann did not seem to hear. He peeked over the rocks. Instantly, bullets skimmed over us. With head down, he raised the red and white Red Cross flag. Miraculously, the shooting stopped. It was my fervent desire to stay hidden behind the wall. I tried to frame this thought as a prayer, *please, God...I want to stay behind.* Well, that prayer went unheeded. Baden started the engine, and we crept out into an open field. Goldmann stood up and waved the flag, hand held over his breast pocket. I knew what was happening. The Blessed Sacrament was there. A British officer called for a cease fire. Immediately, soldiers lowered their guns. I figured they must have thought us crazy. Only crazed men would drive straight into enemy lines. The wooden bridge creaked under us. Once past the enemy, Baden raced off to the farmhouse. Rolf and I made a break for the farmhouse in hopes of finding survivors. Radio messages from the battlefield reported thirty wounded men in the farmhouse. As we neared the farm, a plane swooped over us and dropped bombs. They exploded all around us, leaving smoldering potholes in the path behind us. I don't know how the bomber pilots missed us. It felt like an invisible shield surrounded us. Rolf ran ahead of me into the house and began searching. A young soldier, not much older than me, bled heavily from the wrist. I tore off my shirtsleeve and tied a tourniquet tightly around his bicep to stop the bleeding.

"Help me," he said and pointed to a chain holding a cross.

"Sergeant Goldmann," I yelled.

Goldmann looked like a wild man. Sweat lines ran down his cheeks, now covered in dust. He smelled of smoke from exploding bombs. Like an eagle, he swooped into the room and took command. After checking the soldier's heartbeat, he hoisted the man onto his shoulders and carried him to the wine cellar that acted as a temporary bomb shelter. Goldmann ordered me to stand watch at the cellar door.

"Do you wish to receive Holy Communion?" Goldmann asked the wounded soldier.

"Are you a priest?" he asked.

"I have permission from the bishop," he replied and held up the Host between his dirty fingers.

"This is a miracle. You must be some kind of angel," the soldier said.

"That, I am not. Now, let's say the act of contrition."

During this exchange, I saw movement by the stone wall. Six British soldiers aimed guns at the cellar door. In a loud blast, bullets flew by my arm, tore my shirt, but left me unharmed. A soldier behind me fell dead. I pushed Rolf down and we crawled on our bellies over to Goldmann. For a brief moment, silence fell around us and then I heard footsteps. I peeked out the window and saw British troops marching toward us. We were surrounded with no way out. I tried to pray. *Help me, God. I am too young to die.* It felt like spitting in the wind. The only answer was more British troops. At dusk, the enemy set up camp in a pasture. Our one escape route was the bridge, but two guards were posted. I looked over at Goldmann. His eyes were closed. I guessed that he was praying. My only hope was to trust his judgment.

"Follow me," he whispered.

Under cover of night, we got on our bellies and crept through tall grass. Goldmann picked up a stone and heaved it into brush behind the guards. It was the oldest trick in the book. They ducked down and turned away from us. He threw another stone, farther than the first. One soldier went to investigate. The next stone flew deeper into the olive grove. Both soldiers searched for possible intruders. That was our opening. We climbed onto the bridge and lowered ourselves down into the stream. Hidden by groves of olive trees, we waded toward the sea. On the beach were more enemy soldiers keeping watch. To the east, warships guarded the coast. Goldmann reached into his pocket and pulled out the Blessed Sacrament to protect it from the water. Silently, we waded deeper into the water, up to our necks. With the Hosts held high over his head, we followed the shoreline toward our camp. Just as I thought we might make a miraculous escape, I heard a search plane flying low over the sea. Suddenly, the water was lit by searchlights from the battleships. There was only one escape route. Goldmann held his nose and sank below the surface, still holding the Blessed Sacrament high in the air.

"Rolf, down," I ordered. We both dove under water. I watched Rolf churning in the dark waters, bubbles streaming out of his mouth. It appeared as if he had a smile on his face. For him, life was one exciting game. My lungs felt like they were about to burst. A short time later, the sky was dark. Searchlights were turned off and the plane disappeared. I broke the surface, gasping for air. Stars shone brightly over us, like a canopy of jewels. I thought of Grandfather. On clear nights, he studied the constellations. *Our Creator put them all in place*, he often said, *He has a plan for our lives.* I hoped he was praying for me right now.

Goldmann tucked away the Hosts and spoke softly. "Soon it will be dawn, so we must hurry to shore. Our camp is on those cliffs overlooking the beach."

As waves broke on the sand, a strong undercurrent pulled at my legs, and I was not a strong swimmer. Rolf looked at me with a glint of adventure in his eyes. I held onto his neck and he helped pull me ashore. My boots were filled with water and my uniform dripping wet. Rolf shook water off his fur in a flapping sound. I glanced to the east and saw the sun rising over enemy battleships in a brilliant orange glow. Close to our position were rocks that provided cover. Goldmann gestured for me to follow. For an hour, we climbed toward home base until we spotted German soldiers on sentry duty. They pointed their guns at us.

"Put your hands on top of your head or they will shoot us," Goldmann ordered.

"Who goes there?" the sentry yelled.

"Goldmann and Schmidt."

He lowered his gun. "You survived. Impossible!"

German soldiers under siege are not inclined to smile, but this young sentry did just that. As news spread, men gathered around us offering hot coffee and dry uniforms. Rolf was not forgotten, as one soldier brought him food and water.

"I can't believe my eyes. You are the only ones still alive. How did you escape?" Baden asked.

Goldmann touched his breast pocket. Baden closed his eyes like he was praying.

Chapter 13

Aerial Battle

I watched Johann stand on a rocky ledge and study the sky with his binoculars. Seven days had passed since Bolt was released. Johann took off his cap, his hair wet with sweat.

"How long does it take for a pigeon to fly all the way to Rome and back?" I asked.

"Usually three days.

"Maybe they wanted to let him rest."

"I doubt it."

High overhead, a buzzard circled. Suddenly a black bird appeared. Eagerly, Johann raised his binoculars. Bolt had arrived. The buzzard dove in front of the pigeon and spread his wings, showing the breadth of his powerful body. Bolt dodged in a series of quick moves, but the buzzard closed in, opened his talons and snatched him in one deadly move. Feathers drifted down to earth as the smaller bird struggled to escape, twisting his body. Johann unsnapped the leather case strapped to his waist and pulled out the Luger. With steady hand, he aimed the gun and fired, striking the buzzard in the breast. It dropped like a rock. Bolt spiraled to the ground and landed on the other side of a small hill. Before I had a chance to speak, Johann ran into the open field.

"Stop," I yelled.

Gunfire rang out. Our soldiers thought it was a surprise attack. Hit by friendly gunfire, Johann fell to the ground and tumbled out of sight.

"Rolf, go find."

He bounded out into the battlefield and down the hill. I paced back and forth, trying to squeeze back tears, believing that Johann was dead. As allied airplanes flew back to the aircraft carrier for refueling, our soldiers rested their machine guns on rocks. Goldmann stood next to me, swigging water from his canteen and then offered me a drink. It was the coolest, freshest water I ever drank. Many minutes elapsed before Rolf appeared at the crest of the hill, limping slowly toward us with a strap in his mouth. He climbed over our rock barricade and collapsed in my arms. Upon examination, I noticed a large thorn stuck in the pad of his front paw.

Goldmann moved in for a closer look. "What's the problem?"

I held Rolf's paw in my hand and showed him the thorn. Goldmann paused and then stared at me. It felt like he was searching my face for an answer to his next course of action. The only message written on my face was a trail of tears running down dirty cheeks.

"I don't think he should walk on that thorn. I will pull it out," Goldmann said.

He opened a first-aid bag, took out tweezers and firmly gripped the paw.

"Hold him down. This will hurt."

I hugged Rolf as hard as I could. Expertly, Goldmann pinched the thorn with tweezers and yanked hard. Rolf yelped in pain, but the thorn was out. After cleaning the wound, Goldmann wrapped it in bandages. Without a moment to rest, Rolf stood up and lurched toward the battlefield.

"Looks like he is ready to go," Goldmann said.

"Thank you, sir. I am indebted to you."

Goldmann patted me softly on the back. "Let's get Johann," he said.

"Yes, sir," I turned toward Rolf. "Go find."

Just as Rolf hobbled out onto the field, Baden grabbed Goldmann by the shoulder. "One of our men crawled off the battlefield and is seriously wounded. He needs you."

Goldmann glanced at me. "I can't help you this time. Think you can make it on your own?"

"I have no choice."

He shoved the first-aid kit at me and went off with Baden. I lowered my head and crept cautiously behind Rolf. At the top of the hill, I spotted Johann propped against a rock; he was holding Bolt. Blood stains darkened his sleeve and he looked pale. Bolt cooed softly. Feathers were torn off his side, oozing blood. I turned to Johann and realized that there was no time to waste. I ripped off his sleeve and found a wound in the forearm.

"Looks like you lucked out. The bullet grazed your skin. There's plenty of dirt in the wound so I have to clean it."

"How is Bolt?" Johann asked.

"Not sure. Let's take care of you first."

"Do you know what you are doing?" Johann asked.

"Of course. I have bandaged injuries for months. Now listen, dirt is embedded in the wound and that causes an infection. I have to clean it out. This will hurt. Grab onto Rolf's fur. He will support you."

Private Pigeon Man held onto Rolf while I scrubbed dirt out of the wound and wrapped it in clean bandages. He grimaced but remained silent.

"Here, drink some water," I said.

I lifted his head and put the spout to his lips; every gulp seemed to give him strength. I tied a tourniquet on his upper arm and looped a sling around his neck

"What about Bolt?" Johann asked.

"Let's take a look."

It was strange to see a bird panting like a dog, breathing in irregular patterns, gasping for breath. Blood dripped steadily onto the ground. I used a cloth to put pressure on the injury. Within minutes, the cloth was soaked in dark red.

"I cannot stop the bleeding," I said.

As Johann stroked Bolt's feathers, a buzzard flew overhead, his wings casting a wide shadow over us. Johann raised his fist at the bird and cursed. Bolt stopped breathing and went completely limp.

"I will never have another bird as brave or smart as Bolt," he said.

"Let's take him back and we will bury him, but we better go," I said.

Johann flung his good arm over my shoulder for support and tucked the dead bird in his sling. Months at war had taught me that battles had a rhythm of intense bombardment and brief quiet. Despite the lull, I knew that American forces were determined to kick us while we were down. They would launch an attack soon. Time was running short. Johann skidded down the hill and fell.

"Come on, man. Keep going," I said.

Johann moaned as I pulled him to his feet. Dust kicked up at our feet as we trudged toward the rock wall and in one last burst of strength, we crawled to safety. I settled Johann onto soft grass and buried his pigeon in a shallow grave.

Chapter 14

Mysterious Voices

Over the next month, the 29th Company was on the run, hiding in village after village, surviving as best we could. Most of the farms were deserted so we scavenged for grapes, eggs, and potatoes. One larger farmhouse became a make-shift headquarters where Johann hid out in a basement corner, recovering from injuries. The enemy knew we were here. It was only a matter of time before they would find us. For two days, Baden drove Goldmann, Rolf, and me in the Red Cross jeep, searching for survivors and shelter. One night, we camped out in an olive grove with our backs to a steep mountain. All was peaceful. Rolf lay next to me. I listened to his deep breathing. Sometimes I wished I was a dog. They live moment to moment and never worry. In the distance, I heard the drone of planes and the screech of bombs. The bombardment was swift but devastating. Within hours, wounded men were brought to our first-aid station. After many hours of watching Goldmann, I knew how to dress wounds, and so I tended the wounded without assistance. We worked into the night until all the men were bandaged.

Exhausted, I lay my head on the hard ground and fell asleep.

Two hours later, Goldmann shook my shoulder. "I heard a loud voice. It must be one of the wounded," he said. Reluctantly, I threw off my cover to check on the injured men. All was quiet. We checked with sentries who confirmed they had heard no noises. Goldmann looked puzzled, convinced he had heard a voice. We settled back into our blankets, but he continued to toss and turn. Just as I dozed off, I heard a voice. It sounded like a man's voice echoing in a canyon.

"Wake up and dig. Do it now!" said the voice.

Once again, Goldmann ran to the sentries who only laughed at him. "We heard nothing. You must be dreaming. It is one o'clock in the morning. Go back to sleep."

It is difficult to explain the feelings swirling inside me. I believed this voice was from another dimension. Eyes from another world were watching us. On this peaceful starlit night, a voice from beyond had a message for us. *Do not be fooled. Something was soon to happen. Something bad.* Goldmann leaned against a tree and pounded the bark in despair. His reaction unnerved me. He did not seem to know what to do. Again, the silence was broken. *Dig for your lives!* This time the voice was more ominous.

Goldmann looked up at this sky and called out, "What is the matter?"

No answer came from this mysterious space. I could only sense imminent danger. Like any soldier facing an attack, we grabbed tools and began to dig foxholes. Rolf tilted his head and gazed at me with questioning eyes. Surely, he thought I had lost my mind. He sat and watched us hack the rocky soil with picks. For hours we shoveled, piling mounds of dirt in a fortress around the hole. Rolf yawned in annoyance, but finally he helped us dig. Baden arrived with breakfast for us.

"Forget the food, Baden," Goldmann said. "If you want to live to see your wife and children, start digging."

Dirt sprayed in all directions as we dug deeper into the soil. Now the sun was high in the sky. Finally, the holes were big enough for human bodies. We collapsed on the ground and looked at the cloudless sky. To my horror, I saw ten Allied bombers circling overhead. The pilots must have looked down on us and saw perfect sitting ducks. In one smooth motion, they swept down and dropped bombs. We crawled into our foxholes. Rolf climbed on top of me. Explosions rocked the ground; dirt flew through the air; we were buried alive. I could not move under the weight. It was painful to breathe. I gasped for air. Suffocation was a cruel way to die. Many minutes passed. Suddenly, the dirt above me began to shift. Small openings appeared in the packed soil. Air was seeping through. Openings appeared, until I saw dog paws furiously digging. Closer he came, his legs in a frenzy, creating an ever-widening hole. With my last ounce of strength, I burst out of my tomb. Rolf collapsed on the ground next to me. I hugged him around his scruffy neck. He mustered enough energy to thump his tail against the ground.

The next day, we returned to the deserted farmhouse. Ten men clustered around a table, spreading out maps. Johann emerged from the basement. No longer did he look pale nor did he wince at the slightest movement.

"We heard reports about the bombing. I thought for sure that you were all dead," Johann said.

"It was a close call. War gets crazier every day," I said.

Goldmann did not look up from the maps and said, "Felix, cook up coffee for us. Make it strong. It helps me think."

For the next hour, they leaned over maps, drank coffee, and plotted out our escape from the death trap that was closing in on us. That night we retreated farther north. It was impossible to move during the day; allied bombers would spot us. After many weeks of retreat under cover of night, we moved out of the countryside and entered the eternal city of Rome. A full moon shone brightly, reflecting off the gold dome of St. Peter's Basilica. Germany occupied Rome in September 1943 which made Rome a safe zone for us. Even the Allies would not bomb the Vatican. I awaited orders from Goldmann.

"Take shelter in those occupied apartments. You will find food and drink in the city. I will leave you for a short time to...." he paused and carefully chose his words... "explore the city. Before you do, I have a task. Baden wants photos of all the men in our company. Now stand over there, and I will take your picture."

Johann and I stood shoulder to shoulder against a stone wall. Goldmann aimed a small box camera at us and snapped a photo. It seemed like a strange thing to do as we were on the run, but I ceased to try to make sense of this world. Before leaving, he slipped us money and handed me a letter from an unknown location. My heart pounded as I ripped open the envelope.

Dear Felix,

I hope and pray this letter finds you safe. Three weeks ago, I awoke in the middle of the night with extreme fear for your life. It felt like two strong hands shook me out of a deep slumber. It was not a dream, but an angel warned me to pray for you. Still in my nightgown, I wrapped a shawl around my shoulders and ran to the chapel. I knelt before the tabernacle and prayed with great intensity until I thought my heart would burst. Our chapel bell tolled one o'clock. I prayed, Guardian Angel, save him!

This really happened. I do not know if my prayers were answered.

In Christ's Name,

Mother A

I took off my cap and wiped away sweat: no mention of Willy, and she was careful not to reveal her location or identity. Nazi Germany was still a dangerous country. While I studied the letter, Rolf flopped in the shade underneath a majestic three-tiered fountain. It sounded like water flowing over a rocky stream, bubbling and splashing. Still pondering the contents of Mother Amelia's letter, I strolled over to the fountain. Johann scooped cool water onto his face and sat down next to me.

"News from home?" he asked.

"Remember the strange story about a mysterious voice that told us to start digging? That was the same day, same time that Mother Amelia ran to the chapel to pray." I read him the letter. Johann said nothing. He blessed himself and watched water splash into the fountain.

For the first time in months, I felt an uneasy calm. Even walking through St. Peter's Square, I studied the skies, certain that Allied bombers would appear and reign death upon us. As remnants of a defeated troop, we roamed the city and found small shops selling bread, fruits, and vegetables. After several hours, Goldmann appeared, walking with his head down and looking furtively over his shoulder. That was strange. He acted like someone was following him. As we sat under the shade of a building, he took deep drinks from his canteen, but said nothing. Part of me wished I could read his mind; most of me knew that he was thinking dark thoughts.

"Do you see that red granite tower to our right? That obelisk was moved from the Circus of Nero. In that forum, the Roman emperor Nero presided over countless brutal games and Christian executions. That is where Christians were torn apart by lions, like these innocent people who have died in this war."

After many minutes, Johann broke the silence. "What is that white line painted at the opening of St. Peter's Square?"

"Nazi authorities painted it. According to the Lateran Treaty, the Vatican must remain neutral during war and is a small country onto itself. That line shows where Nazi control ends, and Vatican control begins," Goldmann said.

"Do you mean that anyone who goes on the Vatican side is no longer under Nazi control?" Johann asked.

"That is correct."

A spark seemed to ignite in him. "Sergeant Goldmann, can I speak with you privately?"

They went down an alley and spoke in hushed tones. I saw Goldmann nod his head, take off his hat and they both began to pray. As the huddle drew to a close, Johann blessed himself and walked back out onto the sidewalk but said nothing of their meeting.

This time of quiet in Rome lasted for a week, but then on July 24th, our commander called the 9th Company together for an important announcement. His upright posture was that of a soldier in a military parade. My thoughts leaped in expectation, hoping that the war was over.

"I have news from Berlin. On July 20, a traitorous German named Count Claus von Stauffenberg carried a briefcase into a meeting attended by the Fuhrer. A bomb was inside the briefcase. After planting the briefcase near Adolph Hitler, von Stauffenberg left the room quickly. The bomb exploded, killing and wounding many in attendance. Our beloved Fuehrer survived. The traitor has been apprehended and executed. That is all I have to say. Dismissed."

A bomb in a briefcase! I thought of Goldmann talking in his sleep and of his prayer for courage. This tall medic with studious round glasses was part of a plot to kill Adolph Hitler. Goldmann heard the news without the slightest twinge of emotion. I struggled to maintain my composure. Life was cruel. Hans and members of the White Rose were beheaded as they stood up for freedom. I witnessed the slaughter of German soldiers, some drafted against their wills. Hitler miraculously survived a bomb blast from close range. From a distance, I heard machine gun fire, tank engines revving up, and the crack of sniper fire. I thought of Grandfather polishing Willy's tricycle. I thought of bread baking, of fires crackling in the fireplace. A prayer welled up from the depths of my heart. *Rescue me, God, end this war. I just want to go home.*

Johann walked briskly past me and gestured to follow him. He kept his head down and turned down a maze of alleyways until we came to deserted apartment buildings. In the midst of the buildings were trash cans with lids and rats slinking away from us. Johann sat on the ground and fell silent. Rolf and I sat next to him and listened to the sounds of Rome, of tanks rumbling through the streets and hurried steps of army boots on cobblestone sidewalks.

Finally, he spoke. "I have something important to tell you. Germany has lost the war. It has not been officially announced, but it will happen soon. American troops are on the outskirts of Rome, ready to take back the city. Sergeant Goldmann is helping me escape tonight. Before the war began, I was studying to be a priest. I am taking refuge in the Vatican and hope to resume my studies. Goldmann has connections with a Vatican priest, Monsignor Hugh O'Flaherty, who has been notified that I will cross the white line at precisely nine o'clock this evening."

"If German sentries see you crossing the line, they will shoot you."

"That is why I have a disguise."

He opened up a trash can. Inside was the black clerical suit of a priest, including a black hat with a wide rim. Johann stripped off his uniform and stuffed it into the trash can. In several minutes, he changed appearances from a German soldier to a Catholic priest.

"Looks good on you," I said. "Except that the shoes are too big."

"Only two sizes too big, but they will have to do," He glanced at his watch. "I have to go. Don't follow me. If this goes wrong, I don't want you to be shot."

"How will I know that you made it safely across the line?"

"One clue would be that you won't hear gunshots. Tomorrow, Goldmann will make a small gesture that will surprise you."

"Oh."

Johann held out his hand. "Thanks for saving my life. I will pray for you. Maybe we can meet after the war." Our firm handshake ended up as a hug. He squatted down in front of Rolf and held that noble, furry head between his hands.

"I am grateful to you too, my four-legged friend," he said and rubbed Rolf's ears.

Rolf raised his muzzle and licked him across the nose.

Johann wiped dog saliva away and shuffled off in his oversized shoes, disappearing around the corner. I stood near trash cans in the eternal city of Rome and heard a German soldier yell "Halt!" Johann must have been spotted as an imposter. I had to wait until morning for my answer.

Chapter 15

Journey

One day later, Goldmann sat by the water fountain and ate crusty bread. I sat next to him and opened a brown paper bag containing Italian bread, still warm from the oven of a nearby bakery. To an outside observer, Goldmann looked relaxed, but his eyes darted around St. Peter's Square. I guessed that he was looking for spies who were in search of German soldiers trying to desert. I listened to water splashing on the marble pool and waited for the sign that Johann had promised. Hot sun rays beat down on me, making me sweat. *You don't have to tell me the bad news,* I felt like saying, *I already know that he has been captured.* Still I waited. Still he looked for spies. Finally, Goldmann reached into his pocket and concealed something in his hand. With one swift movement, he slipped it into my pocket. I took off my jacket and leaned over the water, splashing coolness on my face. *When I get the bad news, I will probably black out and fall into the pool,* I thought. With as much casual manner as I could muster, I opened my pocket and saw Johann's black rosary beads. Confused, I looked at Goldmann. He winked at me. I could not believe it. Private Pigeon Man was free; my stubborn heart swelled with gratitude to God.

I whispered a little prayer. "Now, it is my turn to escape."

The 29th Company left Rome and traveled at night through the Italian countryside. Under the light of a full moon, we came to a pasture and stumbled upon a farmhouse. By now, there were six of us left in our military company. Fatigue and hunger gnawed at us. Goldmann knocked on the farmhouse door and was greeted by a peasant woman. Her son, who was my age, stood behind her, holding an ax.

"Please, may we have food and shelter for the night?" Goldmann asked.

She looked at us suspiciously. "Sleep in the barn. There are potatoes in a bin. Here is a basket of eggs, a loaf of bread, and milk. Now, go hide before you are found."

"*Grazie,*" Goldmann said.

It was an old wooden barn loaded with cobwebs and hay, filled with the familiar smell of cow manure. Under cover of night, Baden built a small fire behind the barn and cooked potato pancakes to a golden crisp. Rolf and I made a bed of hay and curled up for the night. Just as I closed my eyes, I heard the shuffling of feet; Goldmann sneaked out of the barn and looked up at the moon. Light bounced off his lens in a mystical way and then he disappeared. With that image in my mind, I fell asleep. Several hours later, someone shook my shoulder. Goldmann leaned down near my face and whispered with urgency.

"British soldiers are coming through the pasture. Soon they will arrive, and we will have to surrender—all of us, but one. Only you will escape. Put on these peasant clothes. Here are fake identity papers made for you while we were in Rome. I made a map on the best route to get home. Here is my Italian-German dictionary. Travel at night whenever possible. Now, go quickly. The British will be here soon."

He gave me a bag of food and shoved money and papers into my hand and then turned to stare out the barn door. I stared at the identity card. The photo was of me standing in front of the whitewashed walls of Rome with a confused look on my face. At this instant, I probably had that same expression. Goldmann took out a gold pyx and held it next to his heart. He bowed his head in prayer. "Dear Lord, keep this child of yours safe from all harm. Guide him in this perilous journey. Now, let us silently call to mind our sins."

I remembered all the bad thoughts that I had about Goldmann when I first met him. I thought about how hatred of God had grown in my heart. *How could God let this war happen? How could God let my grandmother die? Had the Nazis discovered Willy's hiding place?* Grief overwhelmed me, and I sobbed. "God, I am so far away from you. I need your help. If

I have a guardian angel, I need his help. I am sorry for all my sins and beg your forgiveness."

Goldmann raised the Host and said, "*Agnus Dei, qui tollis peccatta mundi, miserere nobis. Corpus Christi.*" At the instant I received the Host, I stopped crying. I felt like a great weight had been lifted off my shoulders. I looked at the tall Franciscan soldier who had saved my life.

"This identity card…you could have one made for you," I said.

"Our whole company could not escape. Allied forces knew we were here and would have hunted us down. Only one man had a chance," he said. "Now, go quickly. I will pray for you."

He turned and left the barn. In the distance, I saw British soldiers marching toward the farm. Goldmann walked toward them with his hands on his head. Soldiers frisked him and aimed their guns at him. *They are treating him like a common criminal,* I thought. That was the last time I saw him.

Hurriedly, I put on peasant clothes and trotted down the dirt road that headed north toward Germany. Rolf looked up at me with eagerness in his eyes. The look in his eyes made me laugh. I squatted and fixed my eyes on his face, "Don't you ever get tired of adventure?" He licked my cheeks. I wiped dog slobber off my face and gazed north. Overnight, my life had changed. No longer was I a soldier in good standing with the Germany army. Now, I was a deserter. If discovered by German soldiers, I would be shot with no questions asked. If Allied soldiers found me, I would be taken prisoner of war. I put that thought out of my mind. For now, I breathed deeply of the air of freedom. I set out along a road that meandered through villages scattered throughout the countryside. Not a lamp was to be seen. All the villagers were fast asleep. Rolf was my sentry. Even the slightest noise would rouse his attention. We trotted on through the night. An hour into our escape, Rolf's ears tensed. A car was coming. I saw two dots of light slowly headed our way. We dove into a ditch and lay flat. The car slowed as it came to our hiding place. I heard men talking in Italian. Something must have aroused their suspicions. The car moved slowly past us and disappeared around a bend in the road.

As darkness faded, we needed a place to hide. The road led us to an abandoned vineyard near a grove of trees scorched by explosions. I gathered handfuls of grapes in my cap and we settled in the forest, eating grapes, cheese, and bread. I opened the dictionary and a piece of paper slipped out. Goldmann had written in Italian the phrase "I am going to Ulm, Germany. How much is it?" The first test of my escape would be the train station. In my many months in Italy, I had learned some Italian words. Under the shade of a tree, I practiced

Italian until I fell sound asleep.

On my first full day of freedom, I awoke to the sound of a bird chirping among the grapevines. It was a small bird with shiny blue wings and not a care in the world. Despite the insanity of mankind at war, birds continued to sing at the rising sun. Grandfather used to say they are praising God when they sing. Birds don't have cares, but I sure did. My canteen was empty, and I had a hole in my shoe; blisters developed on my big toe. I studied my map and surmised that we were 15 miles from the train station. As I contemplated my dilemma, I heard the rattle of a wagon. It was a hay wagon pulled by a horse and driven by an Italian farmer. Cautiously, I emerged from the vineyard. I took off my cap and waved to him.

"Please sir, could we hitch a ride?" I asked in Italian. He did not seem to notice my German inflection, nodded agreeably, and pointed to the back. Rolf and I climbed aboard and covered ourselves in hay. That is how we spent the morning, rocking in the back of the hay wagon listening to the snorting of the horse and methodical clomping of his hooves. If the farmer knew he had an escaped German soldier hiding in a pile of hay, he did not show it. He simply went about his business as if war did not rage around him. That was fine with me. After many hours of bumping along, he dropped us off a mile from the train station.

"*Addio,*" I said.

"*La pace sia con te,*" he replied. We tipped caps to each other and he went off on his peaceful way. As soon as he rounded the bend, I flipped through my dictionary.

"*La pace sia con te* means peace be with you," I said to Rolf who perked his ears at those strange sounds coming out of my mouth. As we limped to the train station, I faced my first real test. A policeman stood at the station with hands in his pockets and rocked on his heels, looking bored. To me, that was a good sign. Perhaps he was just putting in his time and would not scrutinize me. Rolf wagged his tail to show that we were friendly. This must have satisfied the officer who sat down on a bench and opened the local newspaper. We approached the ticket window. I needed to know train departure and arrival times.

"*Dove trovo le informazioni sugli orari do arrivo di arrivo e partenza dei treni?*" I asked nervously.

Fortunately, the man played his role like a ticket machine. I handed him money and he handed me the ticket. As we boarded the train, the policeman put down his paper. My heart raced as he stretched, looking directly at my train window. I yawned in hope that he would not detect my tension. For several agonizing seconds, he stared at me. His eyes narrowed in a way that meant he knew I was not an Italian peasant, yet he made no move. As the train door closed, the engine rumbled to life. With a blast of steam, we lurched out of the station. Rolf looked up at me and thumped his tail on the train seat.

"Maybe we will make it, after all," I said.

My companion in the compartment was an elderly Italian merchant who was returning to northern Italy after a trip to Rome. To my great fortune, he was a friendly man who liked dogs. After a brief conversation about the intelligence of German shepherds, I pretended to doze off – the less time conversing in broken Italian, the better. Onward the train steamed through the Italian countryside, ever closer to home. Our next stop was a border town controlled by Americans. As we pulled into the station, I saw American soldiers awaiting our arrival.

"Security is tight at the border. We will have to get off the train and have our bags inspected." The merchant said. In a low voice, he said, "You are a German soldier returning home. Is that true?" The frankness of his question caught me off guard. I answered truthfully.

"I will help you. Let the dog get off the train with me. You go hide in the bathroom."

Reluctantly, Rolf trotted off with the merchant. After all

passengers climbed off the train, I slipped into the toilet, leaving the door open. The sound of footsteps came closer. I grabbed a coat hook on the back of the door and lifted my feet off the floor. As I held on, a screw holding the hook started to come loose under my weight. All I could do was hold my breath and hang on. The soldier gave a quick look and proceeded to the next compartment. I eased myself down. My hands ached; lines from the hook creased my palms. All was quiet on the train. Cautiously, I opened the bathroom door. All clear. I returned to my seat. I felt a clammy dampness soak through my shirt; my hair was matted and wet with sweat. Confusion reigned on the train platform as passengers bumped into each other, some climbing back onto the train, others leaving. American soldiers chatted with each other, all the while smoking cigarettes and eating chocolate bars. They did not see Rolf sneak back onto the train. Within minutes, passengers returned to their seats. Rolf leaped into my arms and lapped my face. As we pulled out of the station, I looked out the window and saw the merchant disappear around the corner.

With a blast of steam, we slowly pulled out of the station and headed through the Alps that divided Austria and Italy. Cold air of the mountains enveloped the car. Above us were moonlit peaks; silver light shimmered on lakes of the Rhone

Valley. I listened to the rattling of train wheels. The beat said to me, *going home, going home.* As the train rumbled north, I fell asleep, feeling Rolf's warm breath on my cheek. I dreamt of Goldmann praying in a prison cell. *I saw a shaft of light stream through jail bars. Rosary beads dangled from his hands. He appeared thin and unshaven. Suddenly, a muscular man dressed in black appeared at the cell door. He slammed heavy chains against the cell door. "Get up," the man said. Goldmann stood up and left the cell.* I awoke from the dream shaking with fear. As we approached the station, brakes screeched, and sparks flew off the wheels. We arrived at Ulm station, five miles from home where I stepped into the sunlight and breathed deeply of German air. My relief was short-lived. Ulm was a total pile of rubble. Every factory and office building had been destroyed by Allied bombers. Even homes had been destroyed. That meant that innocent women and children had been killed. I remembered what Grandfather had said to me when I went off to war. I remembered him say that war was insanity, that war made men crazy. Never could I have imagined how right he was.

As we walked home, I looked at wheat waving in the field, watched beef cattle grazing in fields and thought how life looked the same in this tranquil valley. Bombers did not attack the countryside. My homeland was preserved, or so I hoped. I thought of the many bike rides I took on these dirt roads with my plump puppy snuggled in the bike basket. Now Rolf was a thin war dog limping home. Pads on his paws were worn down to nothing. My feet had numbness from frostbite in the Russian winter; that numbness stayed with me the rest of my life. We walked all morning until we came to pastures near our farm. A tight knot formed in my stomach. Had my family survived?

"Come on, Rolf. I don't know what we will see. I don't know who is even alive." I braced myself for the worst. Rolf trotted ahead of me, confident that all was well. I walked faster until we came to a ridge near our farm. I saw the stone house and slate roof. I saw smoke drifting out of the chimney in Grandfather's workshop. We ran too fast down the hill and I fell. My face was flat against a pile of dirt. At that glorious instant, I heard the chime of a bicycle bell and jumped to my feet. Willy was busy riding his bike in circles around the oak tree, his blond hair blowing in the wind.

"Willy!" I yelled.

He looked up in surprise. For an instant, he could not believe his eyes, but then he jumped off his bike and ran toward me. It felt like slow motion, this moment of triumph. Grandfather emerged from the workshop with a hammer in his hand. Papa came out of the barn carrying a bucket of milk.

Mama appeared at the kitchen door wearing her floury apron with the big pockets. Try to imagine five people in one tight hug, laughing and crying with tears of joy. In the midst of this jubilation, rosary beads fell out of Mama's pocket. She scooped them off the ground and held them to her lips in a grateful kiss. You need not ponder how I survived the war. Mama showed me the reason. I have more to tell you. Keep reading.

Epilogue

Most people don't think they will ever die. On that day long ago at Grandmother's funeral, I stood at the cemetery, not thinking that I would be buried there, covered over with crabgrass. I died at the age of 83 after a life of training dogs to help blind veterans injured in World War II. I did not go right to heaven but became one of the poor suffering souls in purgatory. It was a helpless feeling; I was unable to get myself out of that place. In this pain of separation from God, I could only wait for someone to pray for me. My children and grandchildren were busy with their lives. They remembered their dear old grandfather as being a good egg, so he must be in heaven.

One day, something happened. A man entered a small country church with white clapboards, a simple church situated in the middle of nowhere. To be exact, it was built on the Great Plains of America, Saint Matthew's Church, it was called. The man's name was Fred. He wore a red flannel shirt, denim overalls, and what Americans called a baseball cap. To Fred, this was no grand moment. He was just making a visit to the Blessed Sacrament before going out in the fields. Just before he closed his eyes, something caught his eye—it was a prayer card. Hmm…he did not close his eyes to pray, not just yet. It was a prayer to Saint Gertrude. It read, *for those who say this prayer devoutly, 1,000 souls will be released from purgatory.* I guess it sounded like a good deal to him. He began to pray. That spiritual grace rose like incense to the heavens. And by the grace of God, I was released and now dwell in heaven.

Heaven is more beautiful than the human mind can imagine. My description of heaven would be another story. I will keep it simple. Upon arrival, I began a project that I never got around to starting back on earth. I wrote down my memories of serving in World War II. That is the story you have just finished reading. You may wonder how it came to be published back on earth. After all, it was written in heaven, and in heaven, you might imagine it would stay. I will attempt to explain by talking about Moses and the Hebrew people. After the Hebrews escaped from Egypt, they wandered in the desert and they were hungry. God heard their plea and sent them manna from heaven. Manna flakes were baked into loaves, like bread. You see, a real object, in this case something you can eat, came down from heaven.

I kept my vow to carry on the work of Hans Scholl, who died to protect our freedom. First, you will need to know a little history. After Germany lost the war, the Soviet Union imposed Communism on East German soil. It was much like Nazi Germany. Communists took over banks, farms, and industry. People opposed to them were thrown into prison camps. Many fled East Germany to escape oppression. In August, 1961, the Communists built a concrete wall between East and West Berlin. The wall was 26-miles long and twelve feet high. Fellow Germans were trapped behind that wall; I took action. Like Hans, I bought a copy machine and wrote leaflets denouncing Communist control of our people. Under cover of night many friends helped deliver these leaflets. We stuffed them in mailboxes and on the windshields of cars. For twenty-eight years, Germans waged peaceful resistance. On November 9, 1989, East Germany loosened its grip and thousands of citizens descended on the wall. I saw photographs of East Germans with hammers and pickaxes chopping down this hated wall. Tears came to my eyes as I read the story. *It was like a miracle*, the reporter wrote. I know what Mother Amelia would say.

Here is one more thing that you want to know. Private Pigeon Man did escape the Nazis, entered seminary, and became a Catholic priest. After the war, he tracked me down and we kept up written correspondence. On one fine day, our family gathered at Queen of Peace Chapel for the baptism of our son. We chose the name Hans Scholl Schmidt.

Real Heroes

Father Karl Gereon Goldmann

Photo credit: Fr. Gereon Goldmann, OFM, *In the Shadow of His Wings* (San Francisco: Ignatius Press, 2000) Page 69. www.ignatius.com. Used with permission.

Father Karl Gereon Goldmann (1916-2003) was taken prisoner by British soldiers and sent to a prison camp in Morocco where he was falsely accused of war crimes. French authorities arrested him and scheduled his execution by a firing squad. Shortly before his execution, Pope Pius XII intervened, saving Goldmann's life. Later, authorities learned of his role in the plot to kill Hitler, thus exonerating him of all wrong-doing. After the war, Goldmann became a missionary priest among poor people in Japan. He established an educational foundation, built churches, hospitals, and a community center. In 1965, the Japanese government awarded him the Order of Good Deeds, the highest honor awarded for social work.

Father Goldmann died on July 26, 2003 at the Franciscan monastery in Fulda, Germany. He was 86 years old. If you were to read more about Father Goldmann, you would discover that many of the incidents about him as portrayed in *Perilous Days* are true.

Hans Scholl

Photo credit: akg-images/Interfoto

Hans Scholl (1918-1943) was a student at the University of Munich when he was drafted into the German army and sent to the Eastern Front. During this time, he witnessed German soldiers committing cruel acts toward Jews in Poland and Russia. After his tour of duty, Hans returned to the university, determined to mount opposition to the war. In the summer of 1942, he bought a copy machine and began printing anti-Nazi leaflets. Along with other students, Hans founded The White Rose, a group advocating non-violent resistance to Hitler's regime. In all, six leaflets were written and secretly distributed. On February 18, 1943, Hans and his sister, Sophie were caught tossing leaflets down an atrium at the university. After brief trials in Nazi courtrooms, Hans and other members of the White Rose were tried and executed. One of these leaflets was smuggled out of Germany and dropped from Allied bombers to exhort Germans to surrender. That leaflet, as written by Hans Scholl, appears in *Perilous Days*.

Colonel Claus von Stauffenberg

Colonel Claus von Stauffenberg (1907-1944) was mastermind of a plot to kill Adolph Hitler. After Germany lost the Battle of Stalingrad in 1943, many German officers in high command came to believe that the tide was turning against their government and that Adolph Hitler was leading them to disaster. They organized a resistance movement led by war hero, Colonel Claus von Stauffenberg, a man who had been badly injured earlier in the war, losing one eye, his right hand, and two fingers of his left hand. As a Catholic, Claus struggled with the idea of killing Hitler, but ultimately saw it as the greater good. On July 20, 1944, Claus entered a conference room carrying a briefcase that contained a bomb. He placed it near Hitler and then answered a planned phone call, allowing him to leave the conference room. The bomb exploded, but Hitler survived. Weeks later, von Stauffenberg was apprehended and executed by firing squad.

Clemens August Graf von Galen

Clemens August Graf von Galen (1878-1946) was bishop of Muenster, Germany during Nazi oppression. In his sermons, von Galen denounced state-approved killing of the disabled. In 1939, Nazis began targeting the mentally ill, epileptics, cripples, and children with Down Syndrome. These programs killed an estimated 200,000 people between 1939 and 1941. As this euthanasia program became public knowledge, Bishop von Galen delivered three powerful sermons that were printed and distributed illegally. Hans Scholl read one of these sermons and declared. "Finally, someone is speaking out!" The courage of Bishop Galen inspired Hans Scholl to organize The White Rose resistance movement.

On October 9, 2005, Clemens August Graf von Galen was beatified by Pope Benedict XVI.

End

Brave Hearts

A Series Featuring Catholic Heroes and Heroines

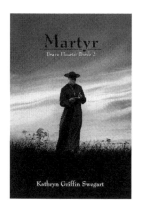

Martyr is the story of a little-known Jesuit missionary of the 1700's, Fr. Sebastian Rale, who lived for thirty years among the Abenaki Indians as their beloved priest. He became the hated enemy of the British who put a bounty on his head.

About the Author

Born in Boston, Kathryn Griffin Swegart earned a Master's degree from Boston College. She and her husband raised three children on a small farm in Maine. Kathryn is a professed member of the Secular Franciscans. Besides being the author of *Perilous Days*, she is also the author of *Heavenly Hosts: Eucharistic Miracles for Kids*.

Visit her website for more inspiring stories.

kathrynswegart.com

Made in the USA
Columbia, SC
09 September 2024

41458702R00074